FEARLESS

Fated Mates – Book Five

Lilli Carlisle

ALSO BY LILLI CARLISLE

FATED MATES
Tigress
Huntress
Speechless
Merciless

THE BLACK RIDGE WOLF PACK
Omega's Choice
Ceva's Chance
Karli's Resolve
Laura's Legacy
Lili's Trust
Katrina's Destiny

www.BOROUGHSPUBLISHINGGROUP.com

FEARLESS
Copyright © 2020 LILLI CARLISLE

ISBN 978-1-951055-99-8

This has been possible only with the love and support of my family.
Love you Craig, Samantha, Katie, and Jason.

FEARLESS

Chapter One

Sarah watched the comings and goings of the small community from the bay window facing the courtyard of the restricted area. It was hard for her to believe she was miles underground. The lighting alone made it seem as though it was midafternoon. The world around her was vastly different from what she'd ever known. She found herself even more on edge than when she was held prisoner by the hunters and demons. Surprising that that was even possible.

Her mind raced back to the day her happy life was ripped away from her. The day the other hyena packs and human-hunters attacked her pack. The ground trembled as the explosions woke her and her family while gunfire erupted around them. Hers had been a peaceful pack unprepared for battle. The smell of acrid smoke seemed as fresh to her today as it had been decades ago. The searing pain from the heat and flames burning at her skin as she fought to hold on to her sister's hand made her flinch even now. Her world swirled into a tornado of fire, smoke, and ash, clawing at her throat, choking her until she lost her grip on her younger sister's hand. Her frightened cries for help were the last Sarah had ever heard from her.

Those cries for help bled into her more recent memories until she found herself locked in her cage at a "zoo," which was really a warehouse for shifters who'd been captured by Collector Demons, vile creatures who'd breached the veil between two worlds with the intention of taking control of Earth. Explosions sounded in the distance as shifters and their new masters, the demons, were all running in multiple directions. Screams for help in unlocking the cages and gunfire punctuated the time between explosions. She'd been chained in her cage when a man appeared, who unceremoniously killed her former keeper with his favorite cattle prod. Typically, her transitions from one master to the next hadn't involved this level of violence, but after years of being a captive, how it happened or when was surely out of her control.

Though, this time around, Sarah had to admit her accommodations were a definite upgrade from the small cage she'd been kept in. Since she'd arrived, Sarah hadn't ventured far from her room without her keeper, a wolf shifter named Joseph—the same man who'd killed her former captor—and she'd yet to ascertain what the shifters Joseph was with wanted from her.

Joseph had backed the couch up to the window so that she could sit on it as she observed her new surroundings. No one had chained her yet, and she couldn't help but wonder when that would occur. Inevitably, it always happened sooner or later no matter who commanded her: demon, hunter, or hyena, she'd been chained for decades. What she hated almost more than being captive was the suspense of waiting to learn what new horror would befall her.

Why wouldn't they get on with it already? She was still waiting for the moment the façade of civility came crashing down. Especially to shifters, hyenas were the enemy and would always be considered a traitor by other shifters regardless of their intentions. In her pack's case, they never hurt another shifter group but, given her kind's history with the wolf shifters, their feelings about her were justified. Hyenas took great pleasure in leading human hunters to other shifters, and had now shifted their allegiance to the Collector Demons, to destroy the wolf packs.

While she waited for the inevitable demands and threats, Sarah had to admit watching the human children play accompanied by their pet dog, Archie, gave her great joy. She could sit for hours watching Jenny and Matthew run around doing this game called tag, or painting, or pretending in a game they called make-believe. Whatever the two got up to was an amusing distraction.

It felt like a lifetime ago when she'd chased her sisters and brothers around their home, playing until they were exhausted. Happiness had been so easy back then when her life was carefree and innocent. Days spent in the valley watching the clouds drift by without a worry in the world. Before she found out they were different. Their pack was different. They didn't behave as other hyena packs, and for their passivity they paid the hefty price with their lives. Sarah was alone in the world without family or a home.

Shaking her head, she tried to shake off the longing for her former home and a life beyond the bars of her cages. Neither existed any longer, only in her broken memories. Surely, her pack would never rise again, so there was no use in dwelling on it. Memories were like explosives. They blew up in your face and tore you apart.

Living in the past was a sure way of getting herself killed in the here and now.

The bear shifter couple, Ben and Marie, who'd helped cut off her chains, appeared to live in this area as well. Along with another bear shifter, Hope, who watched over the rescued human children, there was a woman who barely came out of her apartment. Sarah couldn't help but wonder what they'd all done wrong to be sent into isolation as she had.

Joseph had taken the time to explain that the mysterious woman across the way was named Raine and that she was a human shifter like Ben, but not a bear. He couldn't say which animal she shared her spirit with as the woman had never shifted or given them a clue. Raine even went as far as denying she was a human shifter and distanced herself from everyone.

However, one thing was certain: Raine was beautiful. With her long blonde hair, big brown eyes, and flawless skin, the woman was perfect. Sarah couldn't help but compare Raine's healthy glow with Sarah's patchwork of uneven scars courtesy of past keepers whenever she'd make a mistake or when they took out their frustration on her hide. Any or no reason at all, it was all the same to them.

Even with her shifter healing, the demons had found a way to ensure that she never healed properly. She huffed and shoved the thought to the back of her mind. There was no use in thinking about something that couldn't be changed. Her scars, like her past, would never disappear no matter what she did.

Sarah understood she was a prisoner here, but Joseph had been nothing like the other keepers before him. He'd been kind to her, which was a new tactic in her experience. She knew better than to trust him and his seemingly nice gestures. She didn't trust anybody. Not anymore. For a keeper, he was undoubtedly the best she'd had so far, but that made no difference in the end. She had no free will. Choice was not something that had been available to her for a long time. Sarah wasn't sure what freedom would feel like. Making her own decisions seemed unfathomable after years of captivity.

Apparently, she'd exchanged one prison for another—one master to the next. Sarah had always called the individual charged with keeping her in line her keeper. As in "keep her silent," "keep her muzzled," "keep her working."

She lowered her head to the couch cushions, trying to puzzle everything together she'd seen and heard as Hope came out from her apartment carrying a fabric bag the color of the sky on a bright sunny day. The she-bear didn't stop as she often did when she neared the children, but instead continued in Sarah's direction.

A familiar fear swamped her. Had she done something wrong? Was it time to put her in a cage, or was Joseph sending her away to a new keeper? Hope smiled and waved at her through the window as she neared the front door as if they were friends. Sarah couldn't control her need to run and hide, ingrained as it was to protect herself,

She took off.

Springing off the couch, she ran for the only bedroom in the apartment, passing Joseph, who was getting out of his shower, as she went. That was one of the many things that confused the hell out of her. Joseph would leave her alone unsupervised and unchained. That had never happened to her before. Weren't they concerned she'd try to escape?

"Sarah, what's wrong?" he asked, but she didn't even break stride. Her responses to specific stimuli were no longer under her control. They had become intrinsically part of who she was, occurring without conscious thought, and frustrating the hell out of her. She wasn't a coward, though anyone witnessing her current behavior may find that hard to believe.

The knocking began moments after she managed to wedge herself under the large bed frame and into the back corner of the room, the farthest point away from the door. If they wanted to take her, they'd have to drag her out from under here. Admittedly, she wasn't a large hyena, but she could still put up a struggle if they forced her to leave.

She could hear Joseph opening the front door, letting Hope in. Whatever was going on, he must be part of this. Sarah could hear them talking, but the fear buzzing in her brain made it impossible for her to make out what was being said. The words didn't matter. They never did when they came for her. Another command, another threat if she were to fail were all Sarah would be left with. To them she was merely a tool.

It wasn't long before she heard the door close, which confused her even further. A single set of footsteps were headed in her direction, and by the gait and weight applied to the flooring, it had to be Joseph. When he entered the bedroom, she could scent it was him, and he was alone, making her wonder what was going on and where Hope had gone.

If they followed what had been standard procedure for Sarah's other captors, the bed should be up on its side by now, and they should have been dragging her free of her hiding spot. Sarah dug her claws into the carpet in case that option was still on the table.

Joseph's bare feet stopped at the foot of the bed, and his knees, hands, and his handsome face joined them. She shouldn't care if he was attractive. The aspect of a keeper made no difference. Evil creatures, one and all. Perhaps she was finally cracking under the constant threat of violence and mounting stress. Maybe she had Stockholm syndrome, finding one keeper preferable to the rest.

"It's safe, Sarah. Hope is gone," Joseph assured. She heard no deceit in his voice, and she would know, having had to hone that survival skill over years of being a captive. A slight tone change, nervous tic, or inhalation could be telling. She seemed to average about ninety percent correct, though the number could be skewed as keepers tended to lie.

There was always the possibility that what Joseph was telling her could still be a trick. There was that pesky ten percent when she was wrong. Others had managed to trick her before in a sick game. Some keepers liked to play. They'd offer her hope one moment and then snatch it away in the next after she'd fallen prey to their lies.

While she'd been lost in thought, Joseph had slowly inched his large body underneath the bed frame, forcing the bed to shift up toward the ceiling. Sarah dug her claws even deeper into the carpet through to the underpadding in case dragging her out was his intention.

"I promise no one will harm you here. Hope was kind enough to bring over a few outfits for you in case you wanted to shift into your human form," he continued to explain. "Believe me when I say if someone did want to harm you, they'd have to get past me first, and I can assure you that that's not an easy task."

Sarah remembered Joseph explaining that he was a trained Enforcer for the North Woods wolf pack. At the time, she wasn't sure if that tidbit of information was meant to assure her or warn her if she might try to flee. Considering this new context, perhaps he'd meant to reassure Sarah she was safe. She wouldn't allow herself to fall for it, but accepted that the odds of her comfortably remaining under the bed were slim.

She was sure she'd regret this decision, but Sarah took the chance and inched closer to him, which served to make Joseph smile wider. She watched him for cues of anger and deceit but found none.

"That's it," he coaxed. "It can't be comfortable for you under here."

Sarah couldn't help but feel a bit ashamed and childish forcing him to push his much larger frame underneath here to get to her. A grown hyena should be able to stand her ground, even if she was an albino and came from a pack that was different from the rest of her brethren.

Standing her ground had resulted in painful lessons. Maybe it would be in her best interest to play along. If she didn't cause any problems, she might be allowed to stay here in this apartment for a little bit longer. She hadn't enjoyed this level of comfort since before her pack was attacked by other hyenas and her home was destroyed by hunters.

Growing up, she never knew there was a difference between her pack and the other hyena shifter packs. Her naiveté didn't last long after her eighteenth birthday when the other hyenas and the hunters came for them.

"Would you like to see the clothing she brought for you?" Joseph asked, looking hopeful. He'd been nothing but kind to Sarah since removing her from her cage weeks ago. Perhaps extending an olive branch might be useful. She'd be disappointed when he inevitably betrayed her, but it was sure to happen. For now, she'd play along.

As she crawled the remainder of the way out from under the bed, she didn't think she required clothing. It'd been a long time since she'd taken her human form. As hyena she had more resources to keep herself alive. Her human form was weaker and vulnerable to attack. No shifting, but she could pretend she cared about the clothes since she wanted to remain on her keeper's good side for as long as she could.

Joseph backed out, allowing her enough room so she could follow until they were both standing in the living room once again. The bag she'd seen Hope carrying sat on the coffee table benignly, waiting for her. When Sarah didn't make a move toward it, Joseph went ahead and began pulling the clothing out and holding them up for her to inspect.

While she didn't move, she was drawn to the flowing dresses, shirts, blouses, jeans, and more. Hope had thought of everything a human would need to feel comfortable, which made Sarah worry that they expected her to shift. Shifting was a hard NO for her. She wouldn't give them more power over her than they already had. No keeper had ever been able to force her before, and even in the face of punishment, she'd refuse to do it now.

"Hope said that she wasn't sure about your size in human form and that if the clothing needs to be altered, she has a sewing machine that'll do the job." Joseph looked happy at the finds even though they were not for him, which made her more certain he wanted her to shift. Damn.

The colors of the fabrics varied in a wide range of pastels and whites, which Sarah thought would complement her pale skin and hair. No matter what she thought of the garments, accepting them would be acquiescing to whatever ulterior motives Joseph had.

She didn't do grateful. She'd spent almost all of her life caged and punished. She couldn't muster a thank you for what seemed innocuous, but was probably a trap.

"I wish I knew what you were thinking," Joseph said, sounding wistful before sitting on the couch and looking at her. "If there were a way we could communicate with one another, I believe this transition would be much easier for you. I could answer your questions."

Sarah agreed with him on that point. So far, she'd only been able to communicate with the Goddesses, Raz, Rose, and Zahra. They'd never threatened her, and she sensed they never would. Every one of her previous keepers had insisted she provide them a line of communication, and when she'd refused the punishment had been brutal. To avoid the pain, she didn't see why she shouldn't provide Joseph with the ability to "speak" with her. In the end, it would lead to less confusion, which equaled less punishment.

She padded into the kitchen and rose onto her back legs while bracing her front paws on the edge of the stone countertop. Carefully, she plucked a knife out of the woodblock with her teeth. Once the handle was securely in her mouth, she brought the knife back over to Joseph.

A link would be needed and only used for communication purposes. Her thoughts would remain her own. The exchange of a single drop of blood would open the door to the connection between the two of them alone. If she did the same with the alpha triads, Sarah would have access to the others living here underground. No way was she ready for that, and she hoped they never forced it upon her.

She dropped the knife onto the coffee table and lifted her paw, hoping Joseph would understand what she was suggesting. Sure, she was queasy at the thought of the knife piercing her skin. It'd been only a few weeks since she'd left her last cage in that "zoo." In the interests of keeping her keeper mollified, she was willing to try this much to lay the groundwork for her new captivity.

Besides, she'd already lived through lots worse. Nothing Joseph could do would surprise her.

He picked up the knife, and Sarah cursed herself for the slight flinch that worked its way through her body, but she remained rooted to her spot. She could do this.

"Are you sure?" Joseph asked. "I never want to harm you. However, to have the ability to hear your voice inside my head would be welcome so that I can answer your questions and reassure you."

Sarah lifted her paw higher, showing her acceptance while being honestly curious why he hadn't already forced the issue. When she'd been taken all those years ago, Sarah had shifted into her hyena form and never looked back. Communication with anyone other than her keeper was unnecessary, and frankly unwanted.

Gently, Joseph took hold of her paw and turned it to the side so that he could pierce one of her pads with the tip of the knife. With one final look over at her, he cut his finger and her pad before holding them together for the blood exchange. There would be no telling how long it would take for their link to form, but she knew it was now inevitable.

The big wolf shifter used the hem of his shirt to wipe away the remaining blood from her paw before inspecting the damage. Sarah could already feel the small wound healing thanks to her efficient shifter healing that was now working unimpeded by demonic power. That Joseph seemed concerned confused her. This was nothing more than a scratch that would heal in a minute. He knew that.

It had been a while since someone cared about causing her pain. Apparently, the wolf felt guilty. Wait a minute. The wolf felt guilty. She could feel Joseph's emotions. She wondered if he could feel hers.

His head popped up from inspecting her paw and he stared at her with a wrinkled brow. "You're scared."

She was always scared. NBD. She had reason to be, and keeping her adrenaline up meant she was alert to danger. *"I'm fine."* No need to explain. Usually, keepers preferred when she was frightened. Knowing they held all the power over her was what they desired, coveted even.

He didn't respond to her statement, meaning vocal communication hadn't settled in yet, but he could feel her emotions. She tried to share her confusion, hoping he'd understand that she wasn't sure what to make of all this and what he wanted from her.

"I imagine you're confused by everything that's happening around you, but know that you are safe here, with me," he said, and by his tone, he believed every word.

She wasn't sure if that meant she was safe with him only, and that the others wouldn't be receptive to her being among them, or that she was safe in general. It made sense if the others felt hostility toward her considering the hyenas had sold their souls in order to work alongside the hunters tracking down other shifter species to stay on the hunters' no-kill list.

Though the small albino pack she was born into was not involved in any of that deception, they were lumped in with the whole traitorous species.

She was a prisoner. She didn't have the option to leave if she didn't like who she was living with.

"Hope is one of the kindest bear shifters I know," he said. "If I'm not here and you need anything for any reason, go to Hope."

He was suggesting she was allowed to leave this apartment unescorted. That couldn't be right.

She sniffed at the clothing, noting the soft scent of soap mixed in with Hope's. Faintly, Sarah could scent both children, making her feel a bit of joy that perhaps they'd helped put together the clothing for her. Then she remembered: shifters didn't like humans almost as much as they hated hyenas. Evidently, Hope was the children's keeper like Joseph was Sarah's. That would make sense. Perhaps the human/shifters were forced to endure the same treatment as Sarah. Clearly, they'd been placed in this area to be watched and guarded until a decision was made about their futures.

"You're happy. Now that's an emotion I'd like to feel more of from you," he said before winking at her. Odd that he used a gesture meant to be endearing. She couldn't and wouldn't let her guard down no matter what he did that seemed kind. Tables had been turned on her too many times to believe he was sincere.

It was odd that he felt her joy at the thought of the children packing her clothes, but not the suspicion about the others confined here. Perhaps their link was still touch and go, or he chose not to mention her wariness.

Joseph stood, picked up the bag, and headed toward the bedroom. "I'll put your clothing in your dresser so that whenever you decide to shift, you can come in here and shut the door for privacy while you try them on."

For some odd reason, he had been kind to her since the first moment he'd found her. Why they'd released her from her cage in the first place was bizarre. When Joseph had killed her last keeper, for a fleeting moment she thought she was being saved. Reality set in soon afterward when Joseph warned Marie and Ben as they approached not to harm her.

She was hated.

She was hyena.

Chapter Two

Joseph stood on the thick training mats in the gymnasium with the rest of his enforcer teammates. They'd spent a good part of the day going over maneuvers before practicing on one another until they became proficient in what they'd been tasked with on that day.

There were fifty enforcers in the pack. He'd been one himself for over the past four decades. He'd worked hard to earn his position and had proven himself numerous times over in various battles. John, the bear general, was their newly appointed leader and took no bullshit among their ranks.

Other team members stood nearby or laid out flat gasping for air on the mats. They'd completed the last exercise of the day, and he was looking forward to returning to Sarah when he heard an ugly comment directed at him.

"Hyena lover." The disgust dripping from those two words was what shocked him.

Though it had been said softly, there was no way he could have missed it. Joseph looked over to find the one person he'd least expected to spew that type of nonsense, his younger brother, Solomon.

Joseph stood tall and stretched out his back before approaching Solomon. "You have something to say to me, brother?" He'd take none of this nastiness, least of all from his brother.

If he were smart, Solomon would back down, but today was not to be that day. "You're damn right I do, you traitor. How can you even dare to show up here among us when you're living with a cold-hearted hyena?"

"Sarah is not the same as the other hyenas," Joseph growled. "She was as much a prisoner in that shifter zoo we raided as anyone else we saved. You haven't even bothered to meet her, how can you assume anything about her?"

"How dare you give her our mother's name? What gave you the right to desecrate her memory?" Solomon argued. "Who knows, maybe she was worse than her treacherous brethren, and that's why the humans caged her crazy ass in the first place."

Joseph was getting seriously pissed. He glanced around the assembled men and women to see if they agreed with Solomon's view. He was met with mainly confusion and curiosity. He and his brother had never been at odds before, making Joseph wonder how this animosity came about.

"Our mother would have been honored to share her name with an innocent woman who had been named 'Shame' by those same brethren you compare her to because she refused to help them. It's upsetting to find you've resorted to name-calling and assumptions." Joseph was trying to understand where Solomon was coming from. Yes, hyenas had proven themselves to be untrustworthy, but that didn't mean the whole species was comprised of opportunistic assholes. "It would be the same as declaring all shifters dangerous because they share their life force with a wild animal."

"It's not the same, and you know it. Why would I want to meet one of those?" Solomon asked. "They should all be killed to protect our kind."

"You believe we should kill Sarah?" Joseph looked at his brother, wondering how he'd turned into a vindictive asshole without him even noticing. They may have their differences, but his brother had never been this type of cut-and-dried jerk.

Whatever Solomon was about to say was cut short by the red-faced general. "Anyone want to let me in on what exactly is going on here? Is it you wanted to stick around for some more hand-to-hand combat training?" John flexed his impressive biceps to get his point across. He seemed willing to knock some sense into them over this kind of immature bullshit.

Solomon spoke first, eager to get his point across. "Joseph is living with a hyena. He no longer deserves to be called an enforcer." An accusing finger, stabbed in his direction, accompanied each word his brother spat.

The knowledge that his brother wanted to punish him for caring over Sarah felt like a slap across Joseph's face. Solomon had always looked up to him and followed in Joseph's footsteps to become an enforcer himself. Joseph had raised Solomon by himself after their parents had died. Turning on him was a betrayal he never saw coming, and it was crushing him. Why would his brother do this?

"So, you've made yourself judge, jury, and executioner over the rescued hyena's fate?" John asked, and by the look of anger in the large man's eyes, Solomon might want to rethink his answer. "She's a hyena. Therefore, she's evil and deserves to die without regard to the fact that she's never personally harmed a soul."

Solomon didn't look quite so cocky as before, but he wasn't easily deterred from this path. "Hyenas have caused the death of an untold number of shifters, and we're supposed to accept one here among us?"

John took a few steps closer to Solomon, making the younger man avert his eyes from the more dominant bear. In sharp, clipped words, John growled, "You are to accept whatever your alpha triad has told you to accept. Do. You. Understand?" John's growing canines were bared, forcing his brother to lower his head even further. Being reprimanded was never fun, but having it done in front of your teammates made it sting all the more and guaranteed it would never be forgotten.

"Yes, General," Solomon replied without looking up.

"Anyone else need that clarified for them? The triads have determined that Sarah is not a threat to any of us, and you will accept that," John continued before looking over at Joseph with a wicked smile. "Considering you are in such a hurry to throw away one of our best enforcers for some perceived slight, I'll give you your chance to prove your superiority over your older brother."

Joseph wasn't sure he was going to like what was coming next but was powerless to stop it, much like poor Sarah's entire life.

"You and your older brother are going to spar. First full pin wins, no other rules," John ordered. "Inflict as much or as little damage as you wish."

"What's the prize?" Solomon asked eagerly, disappointing Joseph even further if that were possible. He hadn't raised Solomon to be arrogant and disrespectful.

"If you want your brother out of the group, then you're going to have to pin him down. If you do not, Joseph can have whatever he wishes from you, including your removal from the team."

Instead of backing down as Joseph had hoped, Solomon puffed out his chest in defiance. "Deal. I'll take care of this myself. I'm man enough."

Joseph noticed his brother had glanced off to the side of the gym on numerous occasions toward a woman sitting on a set of bleachers. She must have been one of the evacuees from the zoo or stockyard they'd raided because Joseph didn't recognize her. His brother's weird behavior was out of character, and had Joseph thinking he'd have to look into the mystery woman's identity.

John let Solomon's snide remark go. Instead, he turned to Joseph. "Don't take too long, I'm having dinner with Zahra, and I don't want to be late again."

His younger brother needed to be brought down a few notches, that was clear, and Joseph was the wolf to do it. "Do we fight as wolf or man?"

"Your choice," John said over his shoulder as the remainder of the team cleared off the mats.

"Either form, I'll take you down," Solomon growled.

"What's wrong with you?" Joseph asked. "You've never been a close-minded prick, even when the human shifters came to live among us. Tell me what's going on."

Solomon glanced back at the woman. "My eyes have been opened to the truth."

"The truth? Whose truth?" Joseph already suspected who that person was. "Hers?" he asked as he pointed to the bleachers.

"I'm not here to discuss this with you. I'm here to show you the errors of your ways. If you choose to leave the hyena now, then all will be forgiven," Solomon offered with a cocky grin that Joseph would be sure to knock off his face.

"Forgiven? What the fuck are you talking about? There is nothing I've done to be forgiven." True, it had been weeks since he'd had a chance to spend time with his brother, but his behavior was nothing like the wolf he'd helped raise. "Listen to what you're saying."

"Then you leave me no other choice," Solomon growled before lowering himself to the mat.

"Funny, I was about to say the same thing to you," Joseph countered.

Solomon shifted into his wolf, shredding his clothing in the process, leaving Joseph with little choice. His human form didn't have the benefit of three-inch claws, thick protective fur, or sharp canines.

Solomon attacked first; he'd never had much patience. Joseph easily dodged him while raking his sharp claws down his brother's back leg. It wasn't as severe an injury as it could have been, but a warning that Joseph meant business, and that he was giving Solomon another opportunity to back down, which he didn't take. Of course not.

Joseph squared his body as his brother charged at him once again. This time he didn't move, instead meeting Solomon claw for claw, bite for bite, waiting for his opening. When it came, Joseph didn't even think twice before hurling Solomon into a nearby wall.

Maybe that will knock some sense into him.

Again, his brother didn't take the chance he'd been given to end this and concede. Instead, Solomon pushed himself up onto his four shaky legs and attempted to charge at him once again. Joseph didn't want to hurt his younger brother, he meant only to make a point, which he hoped he'd done.

This time when Solomon came within reach, Joseph dug his claws deeper into his brother's flesh and took Solomon to the ground. Joseph's sharp teeth sunk through his brother's thick fur to barely pierce the skin of Solomon's neck. As his brother fought to break free from the hold, Joseph held on even tighter, waiting for him to tire. He'd never full-on fought his brother before; they sparred all the time, but that was training, this was conflict.

When Solomon finally stilled, John came back over to hover above them. "Pinned, Joseph is the winner. You may demand anything from Solomon, and he will have to agree. He has given his word and accepted the challenge."

Joseph quickly released his brother and shifted back into his human form. Solomon was slow to follow. When his brother glanced over at the bleachers, Joseph automatically did as well to find the mysterious woman missing. Solomon looked dejected but remained silent.

Joseph took a moment and thought about what to demand. He decided it would be too easy to require Solomon to accept Sarah's presence. That would be a statement and wouldn't be real or lasting.

"The only thing I want from Solomon is for him to come over and have dinner with us. Get to know Sarah for who she is and not what some of her kind have done."

Solomon didn't even bother looking Joseph in the eye when he answered. "Fine. But it won't change a thing. Hyenas are all the same. Bloodthirsty traitors. Saving their hides by selling out all other shifters."

John shook his head at Solomon. "Too young and brash. Perhaps the stress and responsibility of being an enforcer for the pack and clan are too great for you."

That statement got his brother's attention. "I have handled all my duties well without a single complaint."

John's voice softened ever so slightly. "Solomon, you need to understand that an enforcer isn't simply all power and strength. An enforcer must have the ability to look at situations logically without allowing their own emotions or others' opinions to cloud their judgment. An enforcer must exemplify all our pack and clan stands for and protect that with their lives if necessary."

Joseph couldn't allow his brother to lose his position no matter how furious he was with Solomon's behavior. "Sir, Solomon is one of the best new enforcers we have. In time, he will grow into a strong leader and protector. I can guarantee it."

Solomon shot Joseph an angry look as if telling him he didn't need his help. He couldn't be more wrong. This little stunt showcased his immaturity, setting off alarm bells with the general.

"Hmmm. I'll accept that for now, but understand I'm watching you, Solomon. In these uncertain times I don't have the luxury of allowing this type of bullshit to carry on among our ranks. Get yourself together or relinquish your position." John turned and looked at the remaining enforcers. "Do I make myself clear?"

A round of boisterous "Yes, sir," filled the large gymnasium.

"Good, keep it that way," John ordered. "Dismissed."

The group scattered while they could. Joseph stood and held his hand out for his brother to take so that he could help him stand, but Solomon refused it outright.

"This isn't over, and some stupid dinner isn't going to change a thing," Solomon growled as he stood on his own. "If you choose her, then I can no longer respect you as my brother and fellow enforcer. You've turned your back on everything we were raised to believe.

You choosing a hyena over me will never be repairable. Remember that."

"I never taught you to be a cold, uncaring bastard. She was a prisoner. She wasn't working with the hunters or demons. That's why she was caged. Why do you refuse to accept the Matriarch's determination that Sarah isn't a threat to anyone?" After the two triads' announcement that Sarah was welcomed here, Joseph had hoped the ruling would quell any residual anger toward her. He had been wrong.

"You believe what you want, and I'll do the same," Solomon growled. "Let me know when dinner is scheduled so that we can get the charade over with."

His brother spat blood onto the floor in front of Joseph before turning his back on him and walked away indignant and having learned nothing.

Joseph didn't know what the hell was going on with Solomon, but he swore to damn well find out. He remained positive in his belief that once Solomon met Sarah, he would realize that she was a victim the same as everyone else in that crazy-ass "zoo." Then they could move past all this internal conflict, focus on shutting the Collector Demons down, and rebuild what was left aboveground.

Chapter Three

Something was wrong. Joseph had been acting oddly over the past four days since his return from training. He was unusually quiet and often sat staring off in thought. Sarah had tried everything she could think of to speak to him through their link, but it still hadn't settled in, which concerned her considering the blood transfer should have worked its magic by now.

Perhaps that why Joseph was upset. Sarah had been able to feel his emotions since the initial blood exchange, and they'd been turbulent and sad since training. She needed to know what was wrong so she could prepare for the eventual fallout, which would inevitably land on her. Whenever one of her keepers had a rough day or was angry, they made sure she bore the brunt of it.

For some unknown reason, she didn't think Joseph would take his frustrations out on her. In fact, he'd stopped her former keeper from tormenting her through the bars with a cattle prod while she was chained in her cage.

Sarah jumped up onto the couch and decided to sit beside him as he continued to flick through some sort of pre-recorded television show. She'd noticed that Joseph liked comedies and documentaries, an odd combination of playful and serious. Today though, he was watching a cooking show for the first time in the weeks they'd been here together, which was weird considering it wasn't as if he had many people dropping by to eat.

She leaned against the back of the couch and whined, hoping he would understand her wish to help, shocking even herself. Her only concerns regarding her keepers' moods had been how they affected her. Since he'd been consistently kind to her, she could at least give him the benefit of the doubt this one time.

Joseph wrapped his arm around her and pulled her closer. "I know it's been a rough couple of days. In truth, I wasn't sure how to deal with this latest turn of events."

Okay, now she was getting worried. What had changed that day in training?

Joseph took a deep breath, and the words rushed out. "My younger brother, Solomon, is coming over for dinner."

Well, that wasn't so bad. Was it?

"Solomon attempted to have me thrown off the team of enforcers, and we ended up fighting one another until I pinned him down."

Not someone she'd invite over for dinner. Sarah was confused, and she assumed Joseph felt her emotions by his next words.

"I know that doesn't make sense to invite someone I fought with to dinner." He looked down at her, and she had the feeling that what came next involved her. Of course, it did. "He believes that I am unworthy of my position because I live here with you."

Lived here with her? Where else would her keeper be?

They'd always wanted to keep an eye on their prize. She didn't understand what was going on around this place, the nuances, and the power structure. Things weren't the way they had been with other captors, and Sarah wasn't sure how to adapt without any knowledge of what was expected of her.

Joseph continued as his voice took on a profoundly sad tone. "He said I need to choose between helping you, a hyena, and him, my brother."

Well hell, she may not understand what was going on here among this mix of shifters, but she knew she was no one worth losing a brother over. They'd assign her another keeper, and she would examine later why the thought of it turned her stomach. So many damn questions. They were piling up, threatening to crush her, and with no way for her to get them answered, she suspected things would get worse.

"I was hoping that once Solomon met you, he'd understand that you are no threat to our people, and as much of a victim of the hunters, other hyenas, and demons, like everyone else," Joseph explained further.

Why he cared what his brother thought of her was beyond her. She was only a commodity, a possession that helped to raise the rank of whoever held control over her. Even if she weren't a prisoner, and free as Joseph had insisted, where would she go? Nobody wanted to be near her kind except hunters and demons.

She pushed hard at their link. She needed answers. Nothing was like what she'd grown used to over the years in captivity. She hadn't been chained or put in a cage. No one had forced her to use her powers yet. Not a soul had attacked her. All that and more should have happened by now.

Growling in frustration while internally screaming for the link to work seemed to be getting her nowhere until Joseph threw his hands up to cover his ears. She hadn't cried aloud. Had she made it through? Was their link finally working?

"Did you hear me?" she asked, afraid of getting her hopes up but needing an answer.

The look of wonder on his face confirmed it before he ever said a word. "Yes, I can hear you."

Finally, their verbal connection had solidified, making her want to cheer. She realized that she hadn't prepared what she was going to say. Great. Now she was mute.

"Please don't stop talking," he requested. "I want to hear your voice. I've been hoping to hear it since I found you."

"Um, hello," she said, feeling like an idiot. Hello? She should've come up with a more substantial introduction. Something a bit more polished so he didn't think she was an illiterate hyena.

"Hello, Sarah." Joseph smiled wide as he spoke. "I'm excited to be able to have a conversation with you finally. You must have so many questions for me."

She did, but for some reason, she couldn't figure out where to start. "When are you going to chain me" didn't sound like a good jumping-off point. Thankfully, he took over when she hadn't managed to string two words together.

"You know you're safe here," he stated. "No one will harm you."

"You have told me this repeatedly." It didn't mean that she believed it.

His expression softened. "I can't imagine how hard that is for you to accept. It will take time. I understand that. How do you feel? I'm aware one of our doctors has checked you over, and there were no immediate health concerns, but are you in pain? Do you need anything? Do you want anything?"

In pain? Keepers dealt in pain in order to control captives like her. They were never concerned with how she felt or if she suffered, as long as she did as they told her. *"I am well."*

Joseph ran his fingers over the scars on her front legs. "I'm sorry that you suffered at their hands. If I could somehow take those memories away, I would."

Was he sorry? There was something weirdly different about this keeper, but she could play along. *"I do not notice them anymore."* Flat-out lie. However, if Joseph knew she was less than honest, he wasn't letting on that he did.

"Where did you come from? Do you have family out there looking for you? Is there anyone we can try to contact on your behalf?" His questions shocked her.

Keepers ask questions, especially personal ones that suggested her family could come get her. Keepers were to be obeyed and feared at all times.

"Southern California originally before my capture. I'm not sure if there are any of my kind or family members left alive." There was no harm in answering his questions, no matter how bizarre they were. It wasn't as if anything else could be taken from her.

Joseph placed his big hand against the side of her head. "I'm sorry to hear that. We could still investigate in case any of them survived the demon attacks."

"Demon attacks?" She wasn't sure what Joseph meant by that as she'd been a captive for many years before the first Collector Demons' appearance.

Joseph's eyes squinted, and brows joined in confusion. "Who attacked your pack, and what do you mean by 'your kind'?"

"Regular hyenas, of course." Was she being tested? *"They came for us. My sister and I. Our pack was different not only in the color of our fur. Our packmates tried to protect us, but there were too many of the other hyenas. Once the hunters arrived, there was no hope of fighting them off."* She was becoming agitated, unsure of the game he was playing. *"Stop toying with me, keeper, please."*

Joseph pulled her closer and ran his fingers through her fur. "I'm sorry I upset you with my questions. I'll ask only one more. What is a keeper?"

***

Joseph could feel Sarah's swirling emotions. Fear, confusion, anger, and uncertainty warred within her, and he hated that he was causing them. Her term "keeper" struck a chord when she'd said it, and he needed to know why she had called him that.

Her body trembled as it often did, and he prayed that someday she'd feel safe enough to gain control over the involuntary shaking. He could feel how frustrated she was by the tremors, but he knew reactions like that were the direct result of severe trauma and may never go entirely away.

"You," she answered with a bite to her voice.

"Me?"

"You are my keeper. I understand the rules. We don't have to play this game. I promise to obey so you won't have to chain me," she vowed.

He wasn't sure how long he sat there in shock. She believed him to be her master. How had he not seen that coming? It made complete sense after what he assumed had been decades or more spent as a captive.

"I'm not your keeper or master. You are free to make your own choices." By the look in her eyes, his explanation was falling flat, and who could blame her for not believing him? He imagined she'd been told many lies over her time spent in captivity.

"Don't toy with me," she growled. *"I have given my word not to run."*

Joseph was beginning to fathom how deeply traumatized Sarah was, and he swore he'd do everything in his power to help convince her that she was indeed free so she could live as normal a life as possible for someone who'd been tortured and abused for as long as she had.

He'd felt a connection to her from the moment he heard her terrified cries from inside her cage. Everything about her drew him closer, and he would protect her even from his brother if he had to.

"I swear what I'm telling you is the truth. I will always tell you the truth. We live underground in these bunkers among a growing number of shifter species, to avoid the Collector Demons and their new human hunter servants. We return to the surface to rescue as many shifters as we can while trying to stop or at least slow the Collectors from taking over. You have met our alpha triads and the goddesses. None view you as anything other than a rescued shifter, and not as any one's servant or prisoner."

Sarah regarded him stoically. *"We shall see in time."*

"Deal. Now let's get back to this dinner situation I've gotten us into." Enough new information for now, it was time to discuss something less stressful, like cooking. *Right.* "To tell you the honest to gods' truth, I can't cook. At least not anything decent. Everything I've brought in for us has been prepared beforehand. I have a reputation for inadvertently starting small fires. On top of all that, I'm wondering why I'm even bothering to try to win Solomon over." His frustration with his brother was reaching a boiling point.

"Because you love him," Sarah answered as if it were obvious.

Joseph huffed out a long breath and laid his head back against the couch cushions. "Yes, I do, but the man I fought the other day wasn't acting like the brother I know. I can't figure out what's gotten into him."

"Perhaps you can find out during dinner," Sarah suggested. *"The two of you can talk in private."*

"If I don't poison us all first," Joseph groaned. "I'm sorry I dragged you into this fiasco. I honestly believe that once he meets you and discovers how wonderful you are that he'd have to realize his preconceived notions about you are wrong."

"I can cook," Sarah offered. Going by his feelings, she figured she was throwing him a lifeline.

"Maybe you can instruct me on what we need and how to prepare it." Then no one will have to visit Jewel in the infirmary. "As long as we take our time, I should be able to pull this off."

"You won't demand me to shift and cook for you?" she asked.

Joseph could feel her uncertainty through their ever-growing link. "No. You shift when you're ready to," Joseph said, hoping that he was conveying how strongly he felt about that. "If it never happens, I'll still be here needing your advice on how to prepare a decent, nonlethal meal."

She snorted, and for a split second, he felt her happiness before it was buried deep once again. He wanted her to be happy all the time, but he was a patient man, and she deserved all the time in the world.

***

"Ready?" Joseph asked as he placed his hand on the silver doorknob.

"As I'll ever be," Sarah replied, desperately trying to calm her frayed nerves by repeating that she was safe over and over again.

"It's not a death march," Joseph teased with a warm smile. "We're simply going to get the food we need to make for dinner. The death march comes after dinner to the infirmary if you leave me unattended in the kitchen for too long." His laughter rumbled from his broad chest as his self-deprecating humor calmed her as she was sure he'd intended.

She had to admit, his behavior hadn't changed in any substantial way since he'd told her that she was free, but it was still too early to know if he was lying and that this wasn't an elaborate hoax. It didn't make sense that he…or they would go to this much trouble to trick her. They had nothing to gain since she was here already, was weaker than all the other shifters, and they had nothing to gain from her. She hoped he was on the level. Any deceit would scar her more now that they'd gotten to know each other after almost a month.

She stood taller on her four legs and fought the urge to turn around as she prepared for the door to open, and for the two of them to walk out of her safe space, side by side. Other than her doctor appointments, Sarah hadn't left the apartment. Even then, Joseph had been forced to carry her because she'd been shaking so badly she couldn't walk.

The click of the latch pulling back was her only warning before the door opened wide, allowing a different hue of light to stream in. She swore she was stepping outside into a real aboveground courtyard, but it was an illusion. The tall metal ceilings were painted blue with a few masterfully painted clouds. The walls were different shades of green blending in well with the potted trees set alongside them, and fake grass that rivaled its living counterpart.

Joseph led the way, and she followed him out. The underground courtyard was full of activity, and thankfully, no one stopped what they were doing to stare at her. For which she was eternally grateful; her nerves were strung tight as a bow.

Marie was lying in a lounge chair reading while Ben worked on some sort of machine on a nearby table. Jenny and Matthew were busy playing in a sheet fort they'd built as Hope watched on. The two tykes had canvased Joseph's apartment for more pillows about halfway through construction. Joseph had laughed and handed them an armful.

The human children didn't seem fazed by the sight of various animals living among them. In fact, the moment Jenny caught sight of them, the child smiled and began running in their direction. Joseph slowed, allowing the little girl to catch up, which Sarah found endearing.

"You finally came out," Jenny cheered before wrapping her short arms around Sarah's neck.

She froze, unsure of what to do. She hadn't been hugged in what felt like forever. It felt foreign, and a little threatening, but after a few moments she began to relax. The children wanted nothing from her, and their affection was pure. If only the same could be said for adults.

Jenny pulled back and ran her hands over the top of Sarah's head. "Your fur is all white. You're pretty. Want to come and play with us?"

"Ah, thank you, and I'm not sure if I'm allowed." Though the offer sounded like the best idea she'd heard in a while.

"Sarah said thank you," Joseph "translated." *"You're allowed to do anything you wish,"* he told her through their link.

"I see you've met the official welcoming committee." Hope laughed as she and Matthew joined them. Matthew, ever the quiet child, might not say a lot, but Sarah had noticed the boy missed nothing.

She couldn't help her discomfort as their group increased in size. She couldn't keep an eye on all of them at once. She was pretty sure the children wouldn't hurt her, but her world had been so uncertain for so long that she couldn't tell the difference between a friendly or threatening situation. In her experience, a threat could come from anywhere at any time.

"I'm Hope," the bear-shifter said. "These two busybodies are Jenny and Matthew." Sarah noticed how affectionately Hope spoke of the children even though they weren't her own, which put her assumption that Hope was the children's keeper in question.

That Hope introduced all of them to Sarah, and in so doing, acknowledging her and not ignoring her as many had done in the past made her a bit optimistic. She'd been a possession for so long that to be treated with fellowship felt good. Weird, but good.

"Hello."

Joseph shared, "Sarah says hello to all of you."

Hope's smile was brilliant and Sarah wondered what she'd done to make the bear shifter so happy. She liked being smiled at and hoped whatever she'd done she'd be able to repeat to get the same response. *"Thank you for the beautiful clothing."* Even if she didn't plan on shifting to wear them, they were a thoughtful gift.

"She thanks you for the clothing. The pieces are beautiful."

A flush went up Hope's neck as she blushed at the compliment. "You're welcome. It was nothing really."

Sarah didn't scent any negative emotions from Hope. Nothing Hope said or felt indicated that Sarah's presence was unwanted. She couldn't help but share a tiny bit of her happiness, making Joseph smile as well.

"It's good to see you," Marie said as she joined them. "I was worried you might never come out."

By her tone, she appeared to be teasing, but this was the same woman Joseph had warned not to hurt Sarah back at the "zoo." *"You warned her not to hurt me when you found me. Is she safe?"*

"Yes, little one. Both Marie and Ben are safe. At the time, I was angry at the man who was hurting you, and I lashed out at them, which was wrong. I've apologized to them for my behavior," Joseph explained. Sarah could feel his shame through their link.

Joseph had been mad at the keeper who'd hurt her?

"Of course I was. No one will ever harm you again." His tone was harsh.

Whoops. I must've thought that out loud.

"So, where are the two of you off to?" Marie asked as Ben joined them, wrapping his arms around Marie from behind her. The love the two shifters shared seemed to radiate off them. It was beautiful to see, while at the same time soul-crushing for Sarah. She knew the odds of her living a normal life with a mate were slim to none.

"We are on our way to pick up a few things for the dinner we're preparing for my brother's visit," Joseph explained. "Sarah's going to instruct me on how to prepare dinner."

At the mention of Solomon, the mood in the group took a definite downturn. Gone were the joyful expressions, leaving concern in its place, making Sarah wonder if this was going to be as awful as everyone else seemed to believe.

"I'm sorry to hear about what happened between the two of you," Ben said. "It's not right."

Joseph looked down at her and smiled reassuringly. "Once he meets Sarah, it will all be in the past."

Sarah looked up at the others and they didn't seem to have the same optimism as Joseph, which worried her. On a brighter note, throughout the entire conversation, Jenny and Matthew hadn't stopped petting her, and she marveled at how calming the simple act made her feel. In this form she felt her hyena's pull almost more than her human's, and her hyena was in heaven and wanted to take the children home. This type of attention and affection was a luxury she'd never been allowed.

"Can we come along?" Jenny asked while taking hold of Matthew's hand. "We promise to be good and to not take a bite out of the fruit before we put it in our bags."

The adults looked down at Sarah as if this decision hinged on her. Joseph confirmed it.

"Is it okay with you, Sarah, if the kids and Hope come along?"

"It's up to me?" She gets to decide who goes where?

"Sure. You have a say the same as everyone else," Joseph responded aloud. The others had heard him say she had a say, and no one seemed shocked by that.

She looked at the hopeful expressions on the children's faces, and she wanted to agree. *"Yes, they can come along."*

"Perfect, we can all go together," Joseph said, making the children cheer and bounce around Sarah in silly little dances.

"That's great. I'll go get my bags so that I can pick up a few things for the kids while we're there," Hope said before turning and walking back to her apartment. Joseph had explained that Hope and the children had two apartments attached and converted into one family home, giving them plenty of room.

"You guys have fun," Ben told them. "I have to get back to trying to figure out how Russo's machine works." He waved good-bye to the children and turned away.

At the mention of that demon's name, Sarah went on alert. Her reaction didn't go unnoticed. Though she wished it had.

"You recognize that name?" Joseph asked.

Was this the test? Trick her into revealing everything she knew about the leader of those dangerous assholes? Which wasn't much, but it was still information they didn't seem to have.

"I don't know anything." Other than that, he was a psychotic asshole hell-bent on their destruction, which they probably already knew.

Joseph knelt and wrapped his arm around her. "It's okay if you don't want to answer. From what I hear, he's powerful and scary."

There was so much she wanted to say about the leader of the demons and his machines, but she couldn't bring herself to do it. Joseph stood and continued talking to Marie. Sarah took the opportunity to take a closer look at what Ben was currently working on. She recognized the machine even though it was in pieces and heavily damaged.

She hadn't intended to move, but the next thing she knew she was standing beside Ben's worktable, and all conversation stopped. This machine needed to be destroyed.

"It must be dismantled so it can't hurt another shifter."

"Ben is hoping to discover a way to make any other machines like this one unusable by the Collectors and hunters. He's quite talented when it comes to technology and can reassemble just about anything," Joseph explained.

"I'm not as good as I'd hoped," Ben admitted. "Every time I think I'm getting somewhere I end up at another dead end with hours wasted. Sarah, do you know about or did you witness anything about this machine that you can share with us?"

Before she could come up with a plausible answer while avoiding the truth, Hope returned with her bags. All ready, let's get this show on the road."

Sarah returned to Joseph's side without comment. She wasn't naïve. She knew they still had questions, and certainly Joseph knew she was dodging Ben's questions.

Joseph shook his head, indicating that Ben should cease his line of questioning.

How bizarre not to be forced to tell what she knew. Not to be tortured until she had no choice but to give them what they wanted.

She was glad Joseph made Ben back off. She wanted nothing to do with that machine of death.

Chapter Four

Sarah had never been down to this level in the bunker facility before. True, she hadn't been in many sections of her new residence, but this one was awe-inspiring. No longer only plain steel walls and floors, but earth and grass, trees, gardens, and more. Flowers bloomed in a rainbow of colors all around her, and the exceptionally tall walls were covered in netting to aid the vines to grow unimpeded.

In the distance, she could make out large plots of land and what appeared to be a substantial hydroponics system. Tiered planters were set on some type of rotating system so that they could be cared for and harvested when ready.

Water tanks bubbled with life as an array of fish swam through tubes that wound around a center section composed of what looked like plants and seaweed. Though there was no natural light this far beneath the ground, an advanced lighting system had been set up that appeared remarkably sun-like, and reminded her of their courtyard.

Everywhere she looked, life was abundant. Sarah could feel her spirits rise considerably by standing among the wonders created here. There were barns and even farm animals in the far distance, and she could hear the distinct sound of a cow mooing.

"This place is remarkable," Sarah said as the children ran ahead with their dog, Archie. It didn't seem as though the children went anywhere without their pet. *"How is all this possible?"*

"It took a lot of hard work and time," Joseph answered. "We were fortunate our ancestors believed in being prepared for any eventuality. Though, at the time, I believe they thought it would be the humans that caused this kind of catastrophic devastation from a nuclear war."

"Hundreds of years went into what you see here, and there is so much more for you to explore," Hope said, adding to Joseph's explanation.

Over to the left stood what appeared to be a modified market with shifters busy collecting goods to stock their shelves. There were shelves, fridges, and freezers. The packaging was different than Sarah remembered store-bought food having. These goods were in plain brown paper or reusable containers and even in bulk bins for a shopper to fill their bags.

How did they keep all of this running? It wasn't as if there was a reliable power grid aboveground left to hook up to, at least ones that weren't operated by the demons and hunters.

"We have underground aquifers we use to generate our power," Joseph answered as if he'd heard her thoughts. Could he have? "Let's go see what's available today and come up with a game plan for dinner." He was approaching this as if preparing a tactical maneuver.

The three of them followed behind the children who'd found a table stocked with boxes of strawberries. Immediately, each of them grabbed a piece of the sweet red fruit and took a bite out of it, breaking their promise not to eat anything that wasn't in their bag. Sarah couldn't help but be concerned that Jenny and Matthew might get into trouble for taking something that didn't belong to them, but the smile on the proprietor's face convinced her otherwise.

There were three wolves and one bear shifter in the near vicinity putting her on higher watch. She knew not everyone was happy to have her here wandering among them. There were those who'd rather see her dead. Sad, but knowing the truth of it had become normal and was expected.

"Hello, Marian, we've come in search of the perfect ingredients for dinner," Joseph said to the older she-wolf closest to them. He lowered his hand to indicate he meant both of them. "This is Sarah. She's going to make sure I don't end up giving anyone food poisoning."

The older woman smiled and drew nearer before finally coming to kneel directly in front of her. Sarah wasn't sure what to do, so she did nothing, allowing Marian to look her in the eyes. Sarah didn't sense any threats, and Joseph hadn't made a move to stop her, so Sarah sat still, gathered her courage, and stared right back.

The older she-wolf's eyes were bright and piercing, leaving Sarah feeling as if Marian could see into her soul. Two much larger wolves came to stand on either side of Marian, adding to the oddity of the situation.

"You've had a hard life, young one. I can easily see that, but your spirit is stronger than you believe. You've caused no harm to any other soul, yet you pay for others' sins just the same. You are welcome to visit this level anytime you'd like. I can always use an extra set of hands or paws, as the case may be."

Sarah tried to remain calm, but the thought of being allowed to visit down here was mind-blowing. She and her family used to have an extensive garden before it had been destroyed along with everything else. There had to be a catch.

"No catch," Marian said, shocking Sarah. "Come by anytime you'd like."

Sarah looked up at Joseph, hoping for an explanation as to why the woman had heard her thoughts. Had their link somehow branched off to include the pack?

"Marian comes from a long line of mages, and she and her mates, Jack and Trek, used to be the alpha triad of our pack until they retired and their sons, Axel and Xander, along with Raz, took over. You've already met them."

A mage was a powerful being, no arguing that point, but this was the first time Sarah had ever met one, and she wondered if they all were able to read minds.

"No, young one, Matriarch Raz is a mage as well." Marian's voice echoed in Sarah's head.

"Wow." So much power in one community. There were goddesses, mages, alpha triads, and more she was sure she hadn't even met yet.

"So, have a look around and let me know if you need any help at all," Marian said while waving her hands to encompass the market area.

"I'm going to go catch up with the kids before they eat themselves into a strawberry coma," Hope said. "I'll meet you guys back here when we're ready to go." She smiled reassuringly at Sarah before heading off in the direction of two laughing children.

Over the next forty minutes, she and Joseph wandered through the pseudo supermarket, searching for the perfect ingredients to impress one angry brother.

"So, ready to help me pull this off?" Joseph asked as he held up his reusable bags. "It's not going to be smooth sailing with me involved. You've been forewarned."

"We should start with the protein." It'd be easier to plan the meal around that.

"Meat it is," he said with a wink. Joseph had a habit of doing that. "The coolers and freezers are this way. We're sure to find something there."

"You do know that protein can come in other forms?" Dairy, soy, beans, and eggs sprang to mind.

"Well yeah, but none that taste as good as beef," Joseph answered as if the choice were obvious, making Sarah laugh at the big wolf.

Sarah had decided it was best to go with the steaks, as Joseph had suggested. She had to admit Joseph was right; every shifter she'd ever known liked steak. When she'd still been living with her family, they would cook red meat often on the grill, and it was always a hit.

"We should grab two large potatoes as well. We'll bake them and load them up with cheese, bacon, sour cream, and chives," she mentioned as Joseph finished wrapping the steaks.

"You mean three, right?" he asked. "You're eating with us. I wrapped three T-bones for dinner." Joseph raised the package as if to prove his point.

Sarah wasn't entirely sure how to answer that. She'd assumed it would only be the two of them having dinner. *"But what if I don't shift to my human form? You can't want a hyena sitting and eating at the table with your brother."* She had no intention of shifting into her weaker form, especially when a person who'd sooner see her dead was coming to dinner.

Joseph squatted down to her level before replying. "Whether you shift or not is completely up to you, but either way, you are most certainly welcomed at the table. Hell, it's our table. If you don't want to shift, don't. I'm happy either way." He cupped the side of her head and scratched behind her right ear, which caused her hyena to melt.

Her damn animal was too soft, soaking up the attention like a sponge, but Sarah's logical side wasn't willing to buy into this dream scenario.

However, she conceded. *"Okay, three potatoes then."* She tried to crush the small but continually growing hope back down. Yet, as time passed, Sarah was having a more difficult time than usual. It wasn't a good sign for her continued safety.

***

Joseph looked down at the ingredients laid out before him on the countertop in utter fear. This wasn't going to end well for anyone's digestive system. Sarah had been sequestered in the bedroom for over an hour, and Joseph knew he'd have to get dinner going soon or it wouldn't be ready in time for Solomon's arrival. He hoped she wasn't stressing about tonight; that was the last thing he wanted.

He'd considered knocking on the door, but decided against it. If Sarah needed time, she'd have it. If she chose not to come out when Solomon arrived, that was fine too. This wasn't about him; this was about Sarah and what she needed.

He chuckled, thinking of how far he'd come since he'd distrusted Marie when she'd attempted to come between their alpha triad. Now she was living happily here in the restricted area along with her mate and others in their small but growing community.

Joseph was thankful he'd changed his mind about the she-bear. Marie had proven herself to be loyal and honest, showing him that someone's actions were not always as cut-and-dried as they may seem at first. When Marie had attacked the bear matriarch, Rose, it wasn't to gain her title but an attempt to end Marie's own suffering. He knew that now.

Mercifully and with grace, she'd forgiven him.

Joseph turned at the sound of the bedroom door opening to check on his little hyena. He was happy Sarah had come out, taking it as a sign she was feeling calmer, but Joseph was completely unprepared for the beautiful woman who appeared before him. He was speechless, and for a few moments they both stood staring at one another from across the room. This was the first time they'd met face-to-face in their human forms.

Sarah was a petite human, tracking being a small hyena. The clothing Hope had brought over fit Sarah well enough. The jeans were a bit long and had been rolled at the cuffs, and the pastel yellow blouse flowed over the stunning pale skin of her albino hyena ancestry, while her thick, white hair barely touched her slim shoulders.

However, what truly stood out to him was her pale blue eyes. He could only compare them to the color of sea glass he'd once seen when on vacation with his family many decades ago. Sarah was absolutely stunning and currently playing with the hem of her blouse and avoiding eye contact.

Slowly, Joseph moved closer, not wanting to alarm her because she already looked like she was going to jump out of her skin. He held out his hand under her sightline, and after a moment, Sarah laid her delicate hand onto his. The contrast between his dark skin and her pale was thrilling.

"You are so beautiful," he said. He wanted her to know not only because he'd promised to tell her the truth, but because she looked so unsure of herself in her human form.

Her blush seemed to be amplified by her pale complexion, making it all the more noticeable. Her free hand tugged at the capped sleeves of her blouse as if trying to pull the fabric down farther over one of the many scars crisscrossing her skin.

Of course, he'd noticed the scars. Joseph wished there was some way he could have prevented Sarah from ever suffering that pain, but those same marks didn't define who she was or her innate beauty.

"Please tell me you didn't feel obligated to shift for this dinner because I assure you that it doesn't matter to me which form you're in."

"No, I thought it would be best to shift so that I can help prepare the dinner," she explained before biting her bottom lip.

"Well then, all I have to say is thank you, thank you, thank you, because I'm so far out of my comfort zone in a kitchen it's not funny. I can be your sous chef. I'm good with instructions, but leaving me in the lead won't bode well for any of us."

Sarah smiled, and Joseph's stomach clenched at the stunning sight. Happiness lit her entire face, making it appear as if her eyes were sparkling. He took a closer look and realized they were.

Deciding now wasn't the time to ask more questions, he packed that away for later. They had a dinner to prepare. Sarah had shifted for him, and that huge concession felt like a victory. He had no idea how to repay such selflessness.

"You can help with the cutting of the vegetables, while I prepare the T-bones and get the baked potatoes on," Sarah suggested as she sorted through their grocery haul, pulling random ingredients out as she went.

In most of the underground apartments, the stovetops had a smokeless grill section because it wasn't possible to go outside and have a barbeque. The facility had been designed with the ability to remain down here for a long time. Their ancestors planned for them to not be able to live on the surface while the world healed.

The industrial ventilation system running through the complex filtered and recycled the air continuously, ensuring that there was never a lack of fresh air for them while living under the tons of rock and dirt.

"Sounds like a plan to me," Joseph agreed as he pulled out a cutting board from the middle drawer under the counter. "I can't mess that up too much, I hope."

"What time will he be arriving?" she asked while reaching for the apron hanging on a hook rack attached to the wall. "I want to time dinner as closely to his arrival as possible so that it's hot and fresh." Sarah began opening and closing cupboards in search of what she needed to pull this off.

"Around seven," he answered. "But knowing my brother, he'll likely be early."

"Six-fifty it is." Sarah nodded as she began pulling things together.

Spices came first, followed by a bowl. Joseph watched as she added different spices to the dish without measuring a thing. Hell, he didn't know anything past salt and pepper. When she was done, whatever Sarah had come up with smelled delicious.

When her hands stopped moving, Joseph looked up to find Sarah staring back at him. She raised her eyebrows and used the whisk she was holding to point toward the empty cutting board.

"We need to get a move on if we want to be ready on time," she said.

Joseph picked up his knife and pulled a bundle of asparagus from one of his reusable bags. "What are we making with these?" He couldn't remember the last time he ate something green.

"We're making cheesy baked asparagus, you'll love it," Sarah said while giving him a concerned look. "You hardly eat any vegetables. That needs to change."

"I'm wolf-shifter. I like meat," he countered.

"Meat is fine, but you need more than that to stay healthy." Sarah was pointing her whisk at him again.

Joseph was so touched that she was concerned about his diet he didn't bother to mention that their shifter health and accelerated healing ensured their continued vitality.

"I get it. That's why we're having these," Joseph said, using his knife to point at the contents of the second bag. Tomatoes, carrots, peppers, lettuce, celery, and other leafy green bits sat there mocking him.

"We're having a salad as well," she said. "But at this rate, we may have nothing to serve," Sarah teased, and then dropped her bowl of spices onto the counter and looked at him with fear written all over her face. "I didn't mean to say that. Please forgive me, keeper."

Joseph laid down the knife he was using and raised his hands in surrender as he neared her. "I am not your keeper. I'm Joseph. You need to call me that. As for the teasing, feel free to do it anytime. Especially now, when I deserve it.

He picked up her bowl and handed it back to her. Now, she wasn't looking at him in fear, but shock. Without saying another word, he winked at her, as he liked to do, and returned to his cutting board and the roughage they'd be having with dinner. Blech.

Slowly, Sarah returned to her preparations, and the two of them continued to work in companionable silence. This domestic scene felt good and right to him, and he couldn't have been happier.

Chapter Five

"I've forgotten the sour cream for the baked potatoes," Sarah realized at the last moment, "and there's no time for us to go back to the market level." He had trusted her with saving this dinner, and she forgot an ingredient. Her heart sank.

Joseph looked away from the salad he was tossing and said, "I bet Hope has some we can use, and then tomorrow we'll replace it. Give me a second, and I'll go ask."

Sarah thought for a moment. Any other "free" person would go themselves. "I can do it."

He looked up again. "You sure? Do you want me to come along?"

She glanced out of their living room window to see Hope and the children playing out in the courtyard. The extent to which this shifter community went to make these apartments look like individual homes amazed Sarah. From the pseudo front porches to the bay windows in everyone's living rooms that looked out onto the courtyard, this place felt like a neighborhood. She had to wonder if the other residential areas of the facility looked the same as this one.

"No, she's right there. It'll only take a moment to run over and ask." She could do this. Sarah wanted her independence, and this was a good test to see if she was truly free.

"Okay, I'll set the table while you're gone," Joseph responded before going back to his salad preparations. No argument or threat, not even a stern look. Huh.

Sarah washed her hands and took off her apron before heading for the front door. She half expected the door to be locked, but it opened when she turned the handle, making her feel guilty for doubting him. The children's laughter poured into their apartment, and she smiled before catching herself. Their joy was infectious.

Deciding to leave the door open, she left the safety of their apartment out into the courtyard in the direction of Hope's place.

Marie and Ben said hello to her as she walked by as if it wasn't a big deal that she was in her human form and out by herself, which bolstered her confidence. It seemed she was accepted here in either form.

Ever wary of the possible fake façades crumbling around her and revealing that it had all been nothing more than a test, she kept her stray thoughts under wraps. When she reached Hope, the woman smiled warmly as Jenny and Matthew came running over to join them.

"It's good to see you out and about on your own," Hope said by way of greeting. "That color blouse looks fantastic on you, but I'll have to hem those jeans."

Not a word about her appearance or the many scars unhidden by her hyena's fur. Hmmm... maybe this will be all right. She'd have a chance to fit in here.

"Thank you for the clothing, they are lovely. I haven't been in this form in a long time," Sarah divulged while attempting to pull the light fabric down farther over her arms to hide the worst of her scars.

"Well, whatever form you choose, you're always welcome in our home," Hope said while waving at the two smiling children. "Jenny, Matthew, this is Sarah in her human form."

Sarah imagined explanations were in order considering they were human and could not scent that she was the same person as her hyena.

"We knew that," Jenny said with authority as only a young child could. "Sarah has the same hair as her hyena." Both of the children came over and grabbed hold of Sarah's hands, unafraid.

The others living in their small community knew her, and she had a real name that Joseph had given her. Such a far cry from her previous existence.

"It's nice to meet all of you...face-to-face," Sarah said and meant it. Before, when she was introduced to someone, there was always a reason behind their meeting, but not this time. Hope didn't want anything from her, and the amount of relief that caused made Sarah almost lightheaded.

"Would you like to join us for some fruit juice and apple slices?" Hope asked while waving at the assorted plates and glasses on the table in front of her.

"Yes, yes, please stay," Jenny pleaded, bouncing at her side. These human children were nothing like some of their adult brethren. Much more accepting and loving.

"I'm sorry, I can't right at this moment, but I'll stop by tomorrow if you'd like," Sarah said before realizing she'd gone ahead and made plans, real plans of her own.

"That would be wonderful," Hope said. "The children and I will make something special. How about lunch?"

Sarah couldn't help but smile at the happy, if not odd, family. A surrogate bear-shifter mother to two orphaned human children who were perfect together. The only must in any family was love, and there was lots of that going on around here.

"That would be nice, but I'll have to check if Joseph has plans first." He may or may not be her keeper, that was still to be proven, but he'd treated her with respect, and she could do the same.

"Great, let me know." Hope's smile seemed genuine, making Sarah smile back. She wanted her to come to lunch, amazing.

"I was also hoping to borrow a bowl of sour cream, please. Joseph's brother is coming for dinner tonight," she explained, "and I forgot to pick some up when we went to the market."

"Sure, I have lots. Come on in, and I'll spoon you out a bowl. Jenny, take Matthew over to the painting area and start on a new picture for Sarah please. You can give it to her tomorrow."

Jenny cheered. "It'll be epic."

"Epic?" Sarah asked, enjoying the little girl's enthusiasm.

"New word, heard it on an old cartoon and now uses it every chance she gets," Hope said with a laugh and a shrug of her shoulders. "Kids."

Sarah followed Hope into her brightly lit kitchen and waited as she took a bowl down from one of the cupboards and filled it with the sour cream. Glancing around, she noticed several stuffed animals with blankets wrapped around them lined up on the couches.

Hope must have noticed. "Movie night last night and everyone wanted to attend."

Sarah couldn't contain her soft chuckle. If these three weren't the most adorable family, she didn't know who was.

When Hope handed her the bowl, she held on to it a bit longer than necessary and looked Sarah straight in the eyes. "No matter what happens tonight with Solomon, you remember that you have worth and belong here. Many among us welcome you openly into our homes. The views of a minority do not speak for us all."

The concern reflected in the woman's eyes didn't bode well for this evening running smoothly. Perhaps Solomon had already made his decision about her without waiting to meet her. Hope released the bowl and led Sarah back to the doorway and out into the courtyard.

"Thank you for the sour cream and your kind words. I will let you know about lunch," Sarah said before heading back to their apartment, eager to finish dinner preparations.

Halfway across the courtyard, two unknown shifters came walking into the restricted area arm in arm. Sarah wondered if this was Solomon, and if so, why would he bring a date? She hadn't made enough for four shifters. Sarah's stomach began churning as her anxiety skyrocketed. The night would be ruined.

Joseph must have felt her emotions through their link because the next thing she knew, he was coming out of the apartment door and straight toward her. The couple stopped when Joseph walked past them without saying a word.

When he neared her, Joseph placed his hands on her upper arms in comfort. "What happened?"

"I think your brother brought someone with him, and I haven't prepared enough food. They will be angry, and the night will be ruined before it starts." Worst-case scenarios had always been her go-to, considering her life had proven them likely to occur.

Joseph glanced back at the couple, and Sarah noticed Hope, Ben, and Marie were now eyeing the new arrivals as well. How had everything turned south so quickly?

"His date can leave," Joseph said, in all due seriousness.

That would destroy any hope of gaining his younger brother's acceptance and not destroying their brotherly bond. "No, I can split my steak with her and throw more vegetables on. I don't eat much anyway."

Before Joseph could argue, Sarah slipped out of his hands and headed straight for their guests. Over the years, she'd learned how to get along with others no matter the situation. She refused to be the reason Joseph was at odds with his brother. She had enough to carry on her shoulders already.

As Sarah neared them, she could already get a read on the woman on Solomon's arm. It was hard to hide outright hatred, and Sarah doubted the woman was even trying.

She could do this.

Joseph caught up to her as she was about to welcome them, but the date beat her to the introductions.

"Is this the way you were raised to greet your guests? By ignoring them as you walk by?" she growled, and that was when Sarah realized the stranger's shifter species. Lioness. Great, as if she didn't have enough to worry about this evening.

It was well-known that lions were a shifter species all unto themselves. Humans would regard them as the "King of Beasts," and lion-shifters took that statement as gospel, thus believing their own PR.

Solomon remained quiet, silently staring at Sarah, making her feel all the more uncomfortable if that were possible. She could feel Joseph's rage, so before he could say a word, Sarah took over, hoping to salvage the evening.

"I'm sorry, a bit of a crisis," Sarah said in a cheerful and pleasant voice. She'd played this game before. "We were missing an integral ingredient." She held up the bowl she'd been holding onto like a lifeline. "Sour cream."

"Sour cream?" The lioness sneered as if the bowl was covered in something contagious.

"Yes, for the baked potatoes," Sarah continued, not allowing the woman's attitude to affect her. "Now, where are my manners? I'm Sarah." She managed to pry one of her hands off the bowl and held it out to be shaken, but the lioness looked at it in disgust and nixed that idea. The she-bitch wasn't making this easy, and Sarah assumed that's why she came along with Solomon in the first place.

Instead, Solomon took hold of Sarah's offered hand and introduced himself. "It's nice to meet you, Sarah. I'm Solomon, and this is Rachel. Thank you for inviting us to dinner."

There were the manners that reminded Sarah of Joseph. His younger brother couldn't be too far gone in his hatred for her. After all, he touched her hand willingly. It did something to a person's psyche when people were disgusted by your touch. The self-loathing was inevitable.

By now, Joseph had calmed enough to speak without growling. "Hello, Rachel. Welcome to our home."

Again, Rachel didn't bother taking Joseph's offered hand. *"Well, isn't she a rude one."*

"Your brother seems nice, though," Sarah said through their link, never happier than now to have it. She suspected Joseph would need to be calmed down a few more times before this evening was over.

"Won't you come in and relax while I finish preparing dinner? Joseph could mix a few drinks while you wait if you'd like," Sarah offered, trying her best to be like the hostesses on those old cooking shows she and Joseph had watched to pick up pointers. How to set a proper table, make basic cocktails, and from which side of their guests to serve. Nowhere in there were tips on how not to strangle an egomaniacal lioness.

"That sounds lovely," Solomon replied, sounding honest, but only time would tell.

"I need a bourbon, neat," Rachel huffed. "I don't imagine you have any?"

"I think we have a bottle of Jim Beam somewhere," Joseph said in a measured tone. "We don't drink much."

"I suppose it'll have to do," Rachel said before walking past them and into the apartment as if she owned the place. Sarah was waiting for the woman to help herself to the fridge and put her feet up on the coffee table.

She caught a nervous smile on Solomon's face in response to Joseph's disbelieving expression before following his date inside. Sarah glanced back into the courtyard to find her "friends" returning to what they'd been doing. Were they her friends? Would they have come to her aid if she needed them?

"You better believe they would," Joseph assured before placing his hand on her lower back and leading her into their home that somehow felt as though it were under attack by hostile forces.

When had she started to believe this was her home?

***

Joseph followed Sarah back inside to find Solomon and Rachel sitting on the couch. Now, if the rude woman could remain silent, they may make it through the evening without bloodshed. This was the same shifter who'd been sitting on the bleachers that day at training when Solomon had called him out for having anything to do with Sarah. When he'd checked into Rachel, there wasn't much to find other than that she'd been rescued.

"So, Rachel," he began, "were you at the zoo or meat packing facility when you were freed?" Joseph knew she hadn't been part of their community before then, so it was a legitimate question.

"The zoo," she growled. "Filthy, disgusting place."

Sarah went into the kitchen while Joseph opened the liquor cabinet over the refrigerator in search of whiskey for the woman. "Sarah was saved from the zoo as well." Maybe some common ground would help this situation. As Solomon remained conspicuously silent, Joseph's frustration grew.

Rachel rolled her eyes and huffed but didn't respond. The lioness was behaving as if she'd been the only one to be caged. That her suffering alone was the primary concern, and Joseph guessed to her it was.

Joseph had been avoiding talking to his brother through their link. Wanting Sarah to remain in the loop, he'd sworn to keep their conversations out in the open. However, it was getting harder not asking him what the fuck he'd been thinking bringing this woman here.

"Aha, here it is," Joseph said as he pulled an unopened bottle of whiskey from the cupboard. He'd picked up a few things when out on topside searches as well as from the stocked warehouses below the market and farm level. "What would you like, brother?"

"A beer would be great," Solomon answered before wrapping his arm around Rachel's shoulders.

"You've got it," Joseph replied, trying desperately not to picture the two of them in any type of relationship. If he were forced to spend any amount of time with Rachel regularly, Joseph was unlikely to keep his mouth shut about her rude behavior.

He pulled two glasses out from the cabinet, put some ice into one before adding the whiskey. Once he was done filling the other glass with a can of beer from the refrigerator door, Joseph walked over to the living room and handed them their drinks.

"You're going to love dinner, Sarah's been busy preparing all afternoon," he praised her hard work. "I would have been more than useless trying to prepare any of this on my own."

"I'm sure we will," Solomon answered. "Besides, if you were cooking, there'd have probably been a fire by now."

Joseph couldn't help but smile at his brother's teasing. This was the man he knew and loved, but his behavior during training still raised questions.

"What are we having?" Rachel asked before taking a sizeable drink from her glass. "This isn't neat."

"Neat?" Joseph asked. He wasn't sure what that meant. The glass was clean.

"Yeah, I said bourbon neat, and you put ice into my glass," Rachel stated while shaking the glass out in front of her, making the ice cubes bang against the sides.

Joseph did everything he could think of to cool down. He counted to ten, took three deep breaths, and yet he was about to blow. Then out of nowhere, he felt Sarah's cooling calm fill him, allowing him to speak instead of yell. "I'm not a bartender. Bottle's on the counter."

"How about we get back to what Sarah has made for us," Solomon said in a rush. "It all smells delicious."

Joseph knew his brother was trying, and for that reason alone, he continued with their prior conversation. "Steak, loaded baked potatoes, cheesy asparagus, a cold noodle salad, and of course, a garden salad." All of which had been prepared for three, he mused. "You'll have to wait a few extra minutes though, Solomon hadn't informed us he'd be bringing a guest, so we're changing a few things up to accommodate." Okay, so maybe it was petty, but he wasn't going to let the rude move slide.

"Sorry, brother. It was last minute," Solomon explained but yet again, Rachel had something rude to say.

"A good hostess always makes more than is needed," she scolded, not even trying to hide her perceived superiority over them, and especially Sarah. "When our chef prepared meals, it always felt like a banquet." Rachel boasted as if that were something to be proud of.

"Around here, Rachel, we don't like to waste food," Joseph growled.

"Please try to get along with her for your brother's sake." Sarah's voice filled his head, calming him instantly. It was becoming a habit Joseph didn't mind in the least.

"I'll go see if Sarah needs any help in the kitchen," Joseph excused himself and walked away before things got any tenser. Gods knew what the lioness would say next.

Who the hell did this woman think she was? Why was his brother even involved with her? Why would he bring her here? This was an important dinner, or at least he and Sarah had thought it was.

"Can I help?" Joseph asked as he came to stand beside Sarah. "Please say yes."

Sarah smirked, knowing full well he'd do anything to stay away from the living room at this point. "Sure, you can add more lettuce and veggies to the salad."

Joseph noticed she was cutting the steak up into thick strips and arranging them on the plates. *"Good idea, splitting up the three steaks like that to share among the four of us."*

"It was all I could think of. She can have my baked potato, and I'll simply have more salad," Sarah offered selflessly.

"You are not going to suffer for their rude behavior. Solomon shouldn't have brought her here."

"Excuse me, will you be a dear and pour me another," Rachel said from directly behind them, scaring Sarah enough that she accidentally cut her finger.

"Shit," Sarah said as she quickly wrapped the tea towel around it. "I wasn't touching the steak, so it's fine. I'll go and bandage my finger up. I won't be long." She walked away before he could get a better look at the wound.

Joseph knew that with their accelerated shifter healing, the cut should heal fairly quickly, but that wasn't the point. This woman's mission seemed to be to destroy dinner.

"What's a little hyena blood between friends," Rachel commented before laughing at her sick joke.

He took the glass from Rachel's hand, sent a scathing look at his brother, and growled, "I'll get you your drink, Rachel."

"Thanks, you're a dear," she said. "Hey, and I respect you taking the hyena in."

"I didn't take Sarah in. She lives here freely." He handed the full glass back to her, sans ice, hoping she'd simply go away.

"Sure, I get it," Rachel said before walking back to Solomon. "We all have that hidden desire to feel needed at different points in our lives. Even big, bad wolves."

At least his brother had the decency to look shocked by his date's words. Joseph was about to check on Sarah when she opened the bathroom door and rejoined him.

"Are you okay?" Joseph asked. "I can finish everything up here if you'd like to relax."

Sarah smiled. "I'm fine. It'll heal quickly, and bite your tongue if by relaxing you mean going over and sitting on the couch with her highness. I'll stay right here, thank you, and make sure to remain alert in case there are any further surprises this evening."

Joseph laid his hand over hers and said, "I'm sorry for all of this."

"Not your fault," she said. "The fact that I'm a hyena will never change, and that angers people."

"I think it's more to do with the lioness's shortcomings than anything you could have done. We'll get this over with, and she'll never be invited back."

"Deal."

Sarah's smile relieved some of his anger, but there was no way his brother was going to be let off for his egregious lapse in judgment. Joseph hoped it hadn't been intentional, and that Solomon would never have done such a thing to him and Sarah. But with only his brother's recent behavior to go by, there wasn't a straightforward answer.

Within fifteen minutes, they had dinner re-plated and on the table. The quicker it was eaten, the sooner they could leave him and Sarah in peace. Gone was any hope of having a meaningful discussion tonight. Rachel was now on her third whiskey and showed no signs of slowing down, unlike Solomon, who still had half his beer left.

Yes, shifters could get drunk, but it took a lot of serious liquor to do the job. Rachel appeared to be headed in that direction on an express train.

"Dinner's ready," Sarah announced as she set the bowl of salad on the table.

Solomon stood and helped Rachel to her feet before joining them at the table. Joseph looked down at the spread, impressed by what they, mainly Sarah, had managed to pull together. No one could find fault with this meal. No sooner had the thought entered his mind, and then Rachel spoke.

"That's all? Where's the rest of the meat?" She sat staring at her plate as if offended by its contents.

"There's steak right in front of you, Rachel," Solomon said, and for the second time this evening, he sounded like himself. "It all looks wonderful."

Sarah glanced over at him before picking up her fork, the concern on her face evident. Joseph wouldn't allow her to think for one moment what she'd done here tonight was less than perfect.

"Everything is perfect, thanks to Sarah," he complimented, causing her to blush.

Gratefully, silence fell as they began eating their meal. Joseph was counting down the minutes until it would be time for them to leave. Had Joseph known it would turn out this badly, he would have never proposed the dinner.

Rachel picked at her food, inspecting every piece before putting it into her mouth. She hadn't touched the baked potato Sarah had so graciously given her, but her whiskey was empty again.

"So, where are you from, Sarah?" Solomon asked in an apparent attempt to start a normal conversation.

"Southern California," she answered with a small smile. Joseph was in awe of her ability to remain cheerful through everything that was being thrown at her.

"Off the streets, no doubt," Rachel mumbled under her breath. Considering they all had enhanced hearing, she knew they'd hear her.

However, Sarah didn't bite at her attempted jab and remained silent. Confirming that by all indications, Rachel was only here to cause trouble tonight. What an awful woman to come along if all she wanted to do was disparage Sarah and start a fight.

"Rachel, please try to enjoy the evening," Solomon spoke calmly, but there was finally some steel behind it.

Rachel huffed but said no more, at least for the time being.

"This noodle salad is so tasty. It might be the best I've ever had." Solomon tried again to compliment Sarah.

"Thank you, my mom—" Sarah began but was cut off by the dinner guest from hell.

"It is fairly good," Rachel said, shocking everyone with the *almost* compliment. Unfortunately, she didn't stop there. "Sarah, have you ever tried some sort of a cream for your little skin problem?" the horrible woman asked as she waved her finger, indicating Sarah's scars.

That was it, Joseph couldn't take any more, but before he had a chance to lose his shit, Sarah spoke.

"I understand that you don't like me, Rachel, and that's fine. But I'm an albino hyena. My kind had nothing to do with what the others have done. We remained separated from them for centuries until the day they came for us, the same as they have for other shifter species." She spoke calmly, never raising her voice.

"Yeah, and I'm to believe that from a hyena?" Rachel laughed. "Lying, cheating vermin."

"No, you're not, but what you are expected to do is sit there graciously like you might contain a modicum of class and enjoy our hospitality," Sarah said in the same tone, and Joseph was happy to see the courage he knew was inside her surface.

"'Our' hospitality? There is no 'our.' This place belongs to Joseph. He took you in like the flea-covered stray you are."

Sarah looked over at Joseph for reassurance, and he'd damn well give it. "This apartment is reserved in Sarah's name. I'm the one who stays here by her good graces. She has more decency in her little finger than you have in your entire body, and I'm more than ready to see you leave."

Joseph reached over and took hold of Sarah's hand in support. This fiasco had gone on long enough.

"You'd kick out your brother for a hyena?" Rachel looked at them incredulously.

"You misunderstand. You're the one who's leaving. Solomon is welcome to stay as long as he likes," Joseph clarified. "At least he had manners."

In a grand show reminiscent of a second-rate soap opera, Rachel stood, knocking over her chair, and threw her napkin onto her plate. She proceeded to down the remainder of Solomon's beer, and when she finally came up for air said, "Fine, but the triads will hear of how disrespectful you were to me."

"Disrespectful. Us?" Sarah laughed, making Joseph turn to look at her. "You came here this evening angling for a fight and have done almost everything in your power to cause it. Do you honestly think they will believe we are the ones at fault? Boy, are you in for a surprise."

Joseph stood and blocked Rachel's view of Sarah the moment the crazy-ass lioness's eyes began to change. If she wanted to go furry, he'd join her, but there was no way she'd make it anywhere near Sarah.

Solomon grabbed Rachel's arm and yanked her away from the table. "We're leaving," he growled while leading the lioness to the door. "I'm sorry for how this went."

Then they were gone. Sarah, still sitting at the table, looked stunned. Then she did something Joseph didn't understand. She pinched her arm hard enough to leave a mark.

"Don't hurt yourself," Joseph said as he went to his knees in front of her, taking hold of both her hands. "It's over. She's gone. You'll never have to see her again."

"I was only trying to wake myself up because that scene couldn't have been real—none of it. I thought for a second I was having a nightmare because I'd been so nervous about tonight being perfect," Sarah explained while looking at the overturned chair.

"Well, it was sort of a nightmare, and her name was Rachel," Joseph growled.

Sarah burst out laughing and wrapped her arms around Joseph's neck. "I don't believe she'll be sending us a return invitation anytime soon."

"If she does, promise to burn it before I see it." Joseph laughed along with her as he held her close.

"I promise."

Chapter Six

Sarah had been lying awake all night trying to puzzle together everything that had happened today. The lioness hated her, that wasn't new, but the way Joseph had defended her, combined with the knowledge that this apartment was hers, was indeed shocking.

She'd chosen to remain in her human form after she and Joseph had cleaned the kitchen and was now trying desperately to fall asleep. Sarah slept in the bedroom while Joseph took the couch. It had been this way since the beginning, even when she was in her hyena form.

The things that Rachel had said weren't new either. Sarah had heard them all her life. Hyenas hated them because they refused to help the hunters, and shifters hated them because hyenas were all lumped together as traitors. She didn't belong anywhere.

"You belong here," Joseph's voice came through their link. *"With me."*

"How have you always been able to hear my thoughts? That wasn't supposed to be part of the blood exchange."

"A bonus, I guess," he offered.

"Only you would consider delving into my mind as a bonus."

"You saying I'm weird?"

"I'm not saying it, I'm confirming it."

They both laughed at the oddity of their conversation. They were only a room apart but chose to talk through their link. Somehow, it felt more intimate. Sarah was beginning to believe she was truly free, which brought with it more questions.

"Let's say you were telling me the truth that you aren't my keeper, and I am free."

"Okay."

"What would I do to contribute?" Sarah noted that no one paid for what they took from the market. Joseph had explained that

everyone was contributing to the group's survival, so there was no sense in charging for things needed.

"Anything you want, or nothing at all. It's totally up to you."

"I can't sit around and do nothing. I have to earn my way." Sarah still hadn't mentioned the reason she'd been so valuable to the Collectors, and that was beginning to feel wrong to her. *"What if I were keeping something from you?"*

"Of course, you're keeping things from me; I would in your position. I may be able to catch a stray thought, but I'm happy I cannot see deeper into your mind. That's your private world, and if you don't want to share that with me, I understand." Joseph had a way of making her crazy thoughts sound normal.

Of all the answers he could have given, Sarah hadn't expected that one. Cajoling her to tell him and reassuring her that her secret was safe with him had been standard procedure for other keepers, which helped to confirm her increasing belief that she was her own person here and not a tool.

"Maybe I will, someday." Sarah never wanted to be forced to watch anyone create a machine of death again.

"I have something I've wanted to give you," Joseph said a bit pensively. *"I originally thought I'd give it to you tonight after we won Solomon over."*

Yeah, that blew up in their faces. *"What is it?"* She was equal parts excited and nervous.

Instead of receiving an answer, Sarah heard something being slid under her door. She sat up to find a small fabric bag with a closed drawstring lying on the floor. Sarah crawled out of bed and picked up the bag, which contained something metallic inside.

"Open it," Joseph said as he stepped away from the door.

Sarah climbed back into bed, and as soon as she got herself situated, she undid the knot, opening the bag. When she poured the contents out onto her hand, Sarah couldn't help but gasp at the beauty.

A shiny silver bracelet carved from what looked like a solid piece of metal slid against her palm. Etchings ran the entire length around the bracelet in the shapes of flowers and vines. It was stunning, and she could feel tears gathering in the corners of her eyes.

"It's beautiful."

"I made it for you."

"You made this?" Sarah was surprised, but realized she shouldn't have been. Joseph had many talents. *"Why are you giving this to me?"*

"Because you are important to me, and I wanted you to have it."

Sarah didn't sense any deceit or a possible ulterior motive coming from him. This was the first gift she'd received in what felt like forever. *"Thank you."* She didn't know what to say that would convey how she truly felt.

"You don't have to explain, sweetheart."

Excitedly she tried the bracelet on, only slightly disheartened when it proved to be too big, allowing it to fall off her wrist and hand easily.

"Give it a second," Joseph said, and moments later, the bracelet shrunk to fit her wrist perfectly.

"How?" That was amazing.

"I asked Matriarch Raz to cast a spell on the metal so that even in your hyena form, you can still wear it, and you won't lose it if you have to shift in a hurry."

Joseph had thought of everything. He had taken the time to consider what would work best for her, what she would like, and her comfort. Sarah's emotions were all over the place, from happy to confused, and a host of others in between. This man seemed to have that effect on her.

Not wanting to say or do anything to ruin this perfect moment, Sarah went with the obvious. *"Good night, Joseph."* She used the tips of her fingers to trace the outline of each daisy and lily.

"Good night, Sarah."

***

Hope and the children had gone all out and had a tea party for their luncheon. Little sandwiches with toppings like cucumber and salmon sat on three-tiered trays; a few were made of metal, while the others were plastic from Matthew and Jenny's toy kitchen.

A large pitcher of raspberry lemonade sat at one end of the table while the desserts sat at the other, rounding out the idyllic summer garden party. Sarah couldn't help but wonder why they would go to this much extent for her.

The children were well behaved throughout lunch with the promise of chocolate cupcakes as an incentive, and were now off playing fetch with Archie's new ball. Marie had brought back a brand-new bag of premium tennis balls on her last mission. She'd even gone as far as asking Sarah if there was anything she could bring back for her. The big bear-shifter turned out to have a heart of gold. Considering Sarah was used to having nothing, she wasn't sure how to answer, so she went with no.

"Thank you again for inviting me over," Sarah said as she and Hope sat in lounge chairs watching the children play. Ben was busy at his table once again, trying to make sense of that awful machine.

"I'm glad you came over after what happened last night," Hope replied. "I'm sorry the dinner wasn't what you'd hoped it would be."

"I'm still unsure why the lioness came over in the first place if she despises my kind so much." Sarah wouldn't want to be near someone she disliked.

Joseph had been called in to speak with the wolf alpha triad and had yet to return, worrying Sarah. Would he be held accountable for what happened last night? Rachel had threatened to go to the triads and complain about Sarah and Joseph's behavior. Would the triads take Joseph away from her? That possibility scared her the most.

"To be cruel is my guess," Hope said while turning to look at her. "There are those who are good and evil in all species, as you know."

"Ain't that the truth." Sarah chuckled. "I couldn't be more of a prime example."

"I'm thrilled we met," Hope said with a smile.

"So am I."

A deep growl caught their attention as they looked over to find Ben holding the sides of his head while staring down at the machine.

"Is he okay?" Sarah asked.

"Physically yes, but he's frustrated and worried that he isn't making fast enough progress on that pile of metal to save other shifters from what his mother and Marie went through."

"They were both put into that cage?" That was horrible.

"Yes." Hope looked at her oddly. "How did you know it was attached to a cage?"

It would be easy to tell her that Joseph had told her that fact, but if she was going to give this a shot, Sarah had to be honest. "I saw it in operation."

Hope's face went pale, and for a fraction of a second, Sarah thought she'd made a colossal mistake.

"I'm so sorry, Sarah. Did they use it on you? Wait, you don't have to tell me anything." Hope looked so upset at the thought of her being placed in the cage that her reaction surprised Sarah.

"I was in it once, when they were testing it." Images and remembered pain assailed her, but she shoved it down. It did her no good to hold onto those memories.

Hope reached for her hand. "If you ever need someone to talk to, I'm always here for you anytime, day or night."

Sarah knew she had to do something to help but feared the repercussions. Would they hate her? Would they fear her? Would they send her away?

"Can we go take a look at it?" Sarah asked.

Hope squeezed her hand and said, "If you want to."

Sarah nodded her agreement. As they were making their way over to the table, Raine opened her doorway and stepped out. This was only the third time she'd seen the human-shifter come out of her apartment. She said nothing to them as they passed, and the woman didn't return Sarah's smile.

"Hello, ladies," Ben greeted as they reached him. "I apologize for losing my patience and growling."

"No worries, you're working for the greater good of all shifters. You can growl all you want," Hope assured him. "Sarah wanted to come over and have a look at the machine. She, like Marie, has first-hand knowledge of its capabilities."

Ben looked horrified. "I should have thought to ask you before I set it out here for all to see. I'll take it to the tool room so that you'll never have to look at it again." He then proceeded to gather up his tools. Marie came out of their apartment more than likely at Ben's distress.

"No. No, you don't have to do that at all," Sarah said. When Ben stopped, she continued. "You truly want to save other shifters by discovering a way to find and destroy these machines?"

"Yes," he answered. "No one should suffer under this machine."

"Not even a hyena?" Sarah had to ask.

"No, not even a hyena," Ben said, and Sarah could feel his conviction. "Especially not you."

She took a deep breath and made her choice. "I wish to help you." Joseph would agree this was for the best for all involved, and she secretly hoped he'd be proud of her.

"Thank you," Marie answered with a warm smile. "Do you know anything that might help us figure out how it was created to drain the life force from other beings to deliver it to a specific demon?"

Here goes nothing. "Yes." Sarah placed her fingertips on the edge of the rectangular-shaped machine and let her powers flow into the metal. The exchange had always felt natural to her, and slowly, piece by piece, the metal reshaped itself back into its original form before being broken.

She increased her concentration once the repairs were complete in order to sense the exact spot necessary. With a slight tap of her index finger, the machine burst apart and hovered above the table in its components, allowing Ben the opportunity to view them separately.

Removing her touch from the metal allowed the pieces to lower onto the table for inspection. "Does that help you?" she asked the suddenly quiet group.

Seconds ticked by, and she hadn't received an answer when an angry scream tore through the courtyard.

"You're a bigger freak than these disgusting animals," Raine yelled from less than twenty feet away. "What the fuck kinda creature are you? A witch or one of those demons they keep talking about? What could Joseph see in you after sniffing around me?"

Sarah couldn't stop her body from shaking. She was loath to admit it, but she needed Joseph. Had she made a mistake? Was she a freak? Her shift was taking over, and there was nothing Sarah could do to stop it.

She was safest in her hyena form in case anyone attacked. Then Raine's final words hit Sarah, "sniffing around me." No one could've missed the venom and intentional slap intimating Joseph had he at one time had his sights on Raine. Talk about bad taste in women.

The next thing Sarah knew, she was standing on all four paws and looking up at everyone once again. The clothes she'd been wearing were either ripped or wrapped around her, making her feel awful for ruining Hope's gift. As she struggled to break free of them, her adrenaline kicked in, and she resorted to tearing the fabric away with her teeth.

At the others' looks of shock, Sarah turned and ran straight for her apartment, thankful she'd left the door open. She didn't stop until she was securely tucked under her bed, a familiar spot. She looked down at the bracelet wrapped around her hyena's right front leg and whined.

Coward. That's all I am, a coward.

***

Joseph skipped the elevator, instead taking the multiple levels of stairs at shifter speed. He'd been halfway back from his meeting with Raz, Axel, and Xander regarding his first apartment and if he still wanted to hold on to it when he felt Sarah's fear, alarm, and self-loathing. Now she wasn't answering his calls through their link, causing him and his wolf to panic.

Nothing mattered more than getting back to her in that moment as he barely felt the stairs beneath his boots as he ran.

"What's wrong?" Solomon yelled as Joseph passed him, but he didn't stop to answer. That would take time he didn't have.

Several flights later, he arrived on their level and tore off down the hall toward the restricted area. If anything happened to Sarah, Joseph would be devastated, and he would make damn sure the person responsible paid.

As he ran into the courtyard, he realized his brother was at his side.

"What do you need me to do?" Solomon offered as he scanned the area.

Joseph could hear a woman yelling, but it wasn't Sarah. Ben was leaning against Raine's apartment door as Raine banged and hollered to get out between loud hissing sounds. Marie and the children were watching from the safety of Hope's front window, and Hope was kneeling on her hands and knees with her head inside his and Sarah's apartment.

Ben waved them over, and it took everything in him not to ignore the man and instead run to Sarah. However, Joseph knew Ben would never stop him if it weren't essential or if Sarah was in an unsafe situation. Maybe it would be best to find out the facts from the trooper.

"Stay by my side," Joseph growled to his brother, who nodded his assurance he'd follow him. They may be at odds, but they were still brothers.

Joseph noted the damage to the loungers, dug-up patches of fake grass, and torn pillows scattered across the floor. "What the hell happened here? Is Sarah safe?"

Ben grabbed the handle of the door as it began turning. "You stay the hell in there until the triads arrive," he yelled at the battered door. "You've done enough damage for one day."

"Solomon, would you take over for Ben, please," Joseph asked so that he could speak to the human-bear shifter without interruption.

"Got it," Solomon answered before taking Ben's place against the door.

"Well, at least we now know what kind of human-shifter Raine is," Ben said. "Believe it or not, anaconda."

"I've never heard of an anaconda shifter," Joseph said in shock. "But I guess she's the same as every other predator species, so it is possible. What does this have to do with Sarah?"

Ben looked away for a moment. "We were shocked. I should have said something before Raine exploded."

"Either you get to the point and tell me exactly what happened, or I swear I won't be able to control myself." Joseph was done waiting to get back to his hyena.

"Sorry, of course. Sarah and Hope came over to where I was working. She asked me if I wanted help with the machine. Of course, I answered yes. Any information is valuable. However, what she did was infinitely better than anything I could have ever hoped for. Sarah simply touched the machine, and it repaired itself. Then she somehow managed to pull all the individual pieces apart and lay them out on the table in order."

Joseph couldn't help but think that was what Sarah had been talking about when she said she had secrets. "Then what happened?"

"We were all shocked, of course, that's an amazing power, but I believe we may have stayed silent too long, making her nervous, and then Raine decided to open her damn mouth. She screamed at Sarah, calling her a freak, witch, and demon and then...."

"Then what?"

Ben took a deep breath before he spoke again. "Raine told Sarah that you'd been sniffing after her and couldn't see what you saw in Sarah compared to her."

"Fuck," Joseph growled and pounded on the door Ben was holding shut. "You better hope I don't get my claws on you, snake."

The yelling and pounding stopped.

"Was anyone hurt?" Joseph asked.

"No, but understandably Sarah shifted and ran back to the apartment. When Raine began shifting into her anaconda, Marie and Hope gathered the children away while I pulled the irate snake back into her room, which wasn't easy. She has to be twenty-five feet long."

More people burst into the restricted area—both triads, Zahra and John, along with four Enforcers.

"Seriously, she's that strong?" Joseph asked.

"The only way I was able to control her was because the shift had disoriented her. I never realized they are that strong," Ben answered honestly.

"An average anaconda can have the strength of at least ten men. Imagine what one with shifter strength can do," Matriarch Rose said as she entered.

Ben looked at Joseph in confusion. "Rose was a teacher before becoming the bear Matriarch."

"Yes, my head is full of knowledge, catch me on trivia night." Rose laughed before joining the others outside Raine's door.

Joseph had heard and seen enough. Without saying another word, he left and headed straight for their apartment and his hyena.

Hope met him halfway. "Sarah won't come out, and I don't want to go in and ruin her safe space."

She looked so genuinely frazzled and upset that Joseph took a second to stop and place his hand on her shoulder. They were all shifters no matter what the species. There was emotional comfort to be found with a fellow pack or clan mates as the case may be. He was a wolf, and she was a bear, but it still counted.

"Thank you for watching over her until I could arrive," Joseph said. "It helps knowing she had someone who cared with her during this time of confusion."

They both turned at the sound of a door crashing open. The three goddesses, Raz, Rose, and Zahra, surrounded the fully shifted anaconda, erecting a barrier between Raine and the rest of them. Her dark green coloration seemed to glow in the lights, broken up by two rows of black spots on her back. She was a thickly muscled snake with a large thin head in comparison to its circumference.

"We want to help you, Raine," Rose said. "Please calm down, and we'll take you someplace your snake would find more comfortable. There will be lots of warm rocks and water for you to swim in."

Joseph understood what they were doing, enticing the anaconda, which was obviously in charge of Raine. He had to admit, she was a fierce-looking snake, and for the first time, Joseph and everyone else felt Raine's terror and fear. She'd been able to hide her emotions in her human form, but now it flowed freely among them.

"Perhaps that's why she was always angry?" Hope said what Joseph had been thinking. "Imagine watching your body morphing into a snake when you didn't even know you could."

"That would mess with your mind," Joseph agreed. "I wonder how long she's been fighting the shift." It was well known that shifting was the most natural occurrence for them, and when fought, it could be excruciating.

Heartbreaking sadness and hopelessness swirled around them as the anaconda lay motionless on the ground with only the occasional flick of a fork-shaped tongue her only movement.

"It's going to be okay, Raine, I promise you," Raz assured as she laid her hand on the top of Raine's large, triangular-shaped head.

"Thank you again, Hope," Joseph said and continued into their apartment, shutting the door behind him.

"Sarah, it's me, and I'm alone. May I come into your bedroom?" He'd never enter without her permission. This was her home and safe place, and he'd do whatever it took to keep it that way.

"Yes."

"Would you prefer to speak through our link?" he asked.

"Please."

"Of course, I would talk to you any way I could." Which was the absolute truth.

"Did you say the same to Raine?" Sarah asked him, and then he felt her guilt for the asking.

"Sweetheart, we have a lot to talk about."

It was time to announce his intentions. He had hoped to wait until she was more comfortable in her new environment, but that wasn't possible now.

Chapter Seven

Sarah knew this day would come. She'd shown them her gift, her curse, and now it was time for her to leave for the cages. The same fear rose inside her, leaving an acrid taste in her mouth.

"Don't you even think that," Joseph said aloud. "You're going nowhere and especially not without me."

"She called me...." Sarah didn't want to repeat the hateful words. Sure, she'd been called names before, but no one had ever compared her to a Collector demon. Was she that bad? Maybe she was and simply didn't know it.

"I know, and you are none of those awful things. You are the kindest, gentlest person I know. Hell, you wouldn't hurt a fly unless provoked. After everything you've been through, you're still fighting and showing an immeasurable amount of strength."

"Strength?" Sarah asked, inching a bit out of her hiding place. *"In case you haven't noticed, I'm currently hiding under a bed."*

"That doesn't diminish your strength in the least. You've come so far, fighting for every inch until you were confident enough to shift." Joseph, it seemed, wouldn't allow any of her accomplishments to go unnoticed. *"You helped me make dinner... Okay, I helped you. Barely. And you had lunch with Hope and the children."*

"They think I'm a freak?" She despised that word. It gave her a nauseous feeling every time she heard it.

Joseph knelt on the bedroom floor before lying on his back beside the bed. *"No one thinks that, and I'm beginning to wonder if Raine even meant it."*

"She said it." Maybe he was sweet on the snake, no matter how hard that would be for her to accept after all this time spent together. Then why was he here lying on her floor next to the bed?

"Yes, she did, but I believe there's more to this story. Fear makes you do crazy things."

"Agreed." She'd done many things driven by fear.

"I knew you'd understand. You have a kind heart. Maybe you can help her."

Sarah inched to the edge of the bed frame. *"How can I help her?"* She doubted Raine wanted her anywhere near her.

"By being the wonderful woman you are. When Raine was a rescue, we brought her here for her safety. Her entire family had been wiped out. From what I hear, her grandmother tried to kill her, but she was possessed at the time. Then on top of Collector demons, dead bodies coming to life, the world collapsing, and a bunch of shifters come along saying they're there to rescue her, she had to be scared out of her mind. Raine fainted when a falcon shifted back into a human in front of her. Her indoctrination into our world was traumatic."

"That does sound bad." Sarah could admit that even a decent person might have cracked under that kind of pressure. *"Was what I did to Ben's machine wrong?"*

Joseph rolled onto his side in order to look straight at her. *"Nothing you've done is wrong. The others were simply shocked by your power. But they are grateful for what you did for them. Now maybe we can figure out a way to stop those machines from being used by the demons."*

"I was in the cage once," she admitted.

"They used that machine on you?" His voice became deadly, but Sarah knew his anger wasn't directed at her but her captors.

"Yes, but they later decided I was more useful for my talents and stopped."

"Can you explain your powers to me?" Joseph asked as he reached out his hand to her.

Sarah scooted the remaining way from under the bed and curled her hyena body against Joseph's side. *"I'm psychokinetic. I can move things, return items to their original form, take things apart, and so on with my mind."*

"That is amazing. I wish I had some sort of ability."

"No, you don't. People hunt you down and want to use you to better themselves. To control you and your ability." No one deserved to live like that.

"Is that why the hyenas came for you and your sister?"

"Yes. Word had gotten out of our small pack, and they came for us. They killed every other pack member so that there was no one left to try to rescue us." The memories attacked her unbidden. The smoke and gunfire assailed her senses as if they were real.

"Do you know where your sister is now?" Joseph asked. *"Does she have the same ability as you do?"*

"She has a different effect on the world around her than myself. She can animate inanimate objects to do as she asks. They separated us almost immediately. I never saw her again after the initial attack."

Joseph wrapped his other arm around her and held her close as they lay on the floor. "We will try to find her, I swear."

"I've tried many times to reach her through our link as sisters, but I've never received a response." Sarah had prayed her sister hadn't gone through with her plan to end her own life. Unfortunately, if she did, though Sarah would be devastated, she could also understand.

"What is your sister's name? We can send out feelers to other shifter compounds. We have contacts all over the globe."

"We didn't have our names yet. Our people performed a sacred ceremony on each member's nineteenth birthday, where they were able to choose their names. We were taken at eighteen."

"Is that why you told us your name was 'Shame'?"

"Yes, that is what the other hyenas had named me."

"Do you like the name Sarah?" Joseph asked. *"If not, you can change it to whatever you'd like."*

"I like my new name. I wish to keep it." He had given it to her on the day he'd saved her.

"Tomorrow, we'll go talk with the alpha triad and give them as much detail as we can so that the search can begin."

Sarah raised her hyena's head. *"You will help me find my sister?"*

"Yes."

"Thank you."

Sarah laid her head back down on Joseph's muscled arm, trying her hardest to stop herself from asking the question that was front and center in her mind.

"No, Raine and I didn't have a relationship. I visited her once, and that was all. If you want the truth, I'd like to stay here with you, if you'll let me."

Sarah imagined a reality without Joseph by her side, and she didn't like it. *"That would be okay with me."*

"Good," Joseph replied. *"How about I lift you onto the mattress so that you can rest for a while?"*

"Will you stay with me?" she asked before she realized she was going to say the words.

"I'll be wherever you need me to be," Joseph said before sitting up and taking her into his arms. Her hyena seemed so small compared to him. He laid her down on the far side of the bed and placed himself between the bedroom door and her. Ever her guardian.

"Rest now. There is nothing for you to worry about here, I promise." Joseph's voice was soothing.

Sarah wished more than anything for his words to be true. Worrying had kept her alive, and it would be hard for her to let that go.

***

The boardroom looked as menacing as it sounded when Joseph had informed her of their meeting with the triads. She tried to sit still in her chair, but her nervous energy was getting the better of her. Twisting her fingers, though painful, was a good distraction as they waited.

Joseph reached over from his chair and took hold of her hand. "I swear there is nothing for you to worry over. Our leaders are good and fair people, and only wish to help you."

"I believe you," Sarah assured. "Worry is a built-in automatic response."

"In that case, I will take it upon myself to reassure you every day, so that you can build new responses to situations," Joseph promised.

Sarah liked the sound of that. She spent so much energy daily being on constant alert with her flight-or-fight instinct in a continual loop, she was exhausted. Over the last few weeks, she'd allowed herself a few moments of joy, and she wished to continue learning how to extend those times.

She couldn't help her small jump when the exterior doors opened, revealing the same shifters she'd met a few days after her arrival. As well as Zahra and John, who had come to visit her on the first night.

"Hello, again, Sarah," Raz said. "It is so nice to be able to put a face to your beautiful hyena."

Zahra and John came around the table and sat on either side of them, making Sarah a touch nervous until the Goddess reached out and held her hand, filling her with calm. *"You are safe here with us."* It always amazed Sarah that Zahra could talk even without having a physical voice. Her words came through the air for all to hear.

With her left hand in Joseph's hand and her right in Zahra's, Sarah thought she might be able to get through this. The other six took their seats, and Sarah couldn't find an ounce of anger among them, which helped her to remain in her chair.

"We understand that you have a sister you would like to find?" Alpha Axel asked.

"Yes, please, sir." More than anything.

"You may call me alpha or Axel, your choice, but we're a family here all trying to survive while saving as many as we can along the way. Sir sounds way too formal," Axel said with a warm smile.

"Yes, sir… I mean, alpha." Weird, but okay. Usually, the people in charge wanted to be distinguished from the rest.

"Would you allow Matriarch Rose to look through your memories of your sister? It will be much quicker and far easier that way, and then she can share with us," Alpha Mason asked.

That surprised her. When they'd found her, they hadn't made her join the communal link shared among all members in the bunker system. This was the first time one of them—except Joseph and the mages—would be in her mind.

"Yes, that would be fine," she responded while trying to keep the quiver from her voice.

Rose stood and walked over to stand behind Sarah's chair. Her smile was reassuring, and Sarah sensed no malice.

"Ready?" Rose asked. "I promise this won't hurt even the tiniest."

Sarah nodded her head, closed her eyes, and concentrated on her sister as Rose placed her hands on top of Sarah's head. Everything she could remember and a few things she'd forgotten flooded back. Like the way her sister always wore her hair in a ponytail, or her addiction to watermelon. Anything Sarah could think of, whether it was crucial or not, she tried to summon.

"Thank you, Sarah," Rose said before removing her hands and walking back to her seat between her mates Mason and Riker.

Joseph squeezed her hand, and she took a deep, calming breath. It was going to be okay. These shifters had been good and kind to her, and she was beginning to doubt that would ever change.

"You gave us a lot of information to go on, Sarah," Beta Riker said. "This will help us begin the search."

Sarah let out a breath she hadn't realized she'd been holding. "Thank you. Thank all of you." They were going to help her, and even though there was no guarantee they'd find her sister, they were willing to try. For Sarah.

Axel's expression became serious. "I imagine we should discuss the other reason for this meeting."

Sarah's smile vanished.

"We have been made aware of your abilities, and we would like to discuss that with you now. Is that okay with you?" Axel asked.

They were asking her, not forcing her. Crucial difference.

"Yes, I will answer your questions to the best of my ability," Sarah agreed, while squeezing Joseph's hand tighter.

"That's all we can ask," Zahra said as she squeezed Sarah's other hand. Since her pack was attacked and destroyed, she'd never experience this type of support from other shifters. When she'd been a captive, the other imprisoned shifters were busy trying to stay alive. Support wasn't even on their radar.

"From what we've been told, you can do amazing things with your mind and touch," Raz stated. "Could you explain this to us, please?"

"I'm psychokinetic. I can move, transform, and manipulate objects." Hummingbirds' beating wings lifted off in her stomach. Her secret was well and truly out.

"You used this ability to help Ben with the machine that was recovered from the packing facility, correct?" Riker asked.

"Yes. I repaired it and then dismantled it so that Ben can discover a way to destroy the others." Which was crucial in her mind.

"Are there many others?" Xander asked, his concern evident by his stoic tone.

"I wasn't allowed the freedom to count, but the day they put me in that cage, I noticed a group of them on a nearby table," Sarah answered truthfully. She'd been terrified.

"Do you know where they went?" Rose asked. "Or to whom?"

"No," Sarah replied, then thought there might be another way to find out. "However, I can guarantee wherever they are, you should be able to find a spike in electricity in that same area. Typically, they'd siphon the electricity from the surrounding towns, if there was any left to be found, and redirect it into the machine."

The alpha triads glanced at one another while surely discussing this information through their private link.

"That's going to help us greatly. Once Ben figures out how we can turn them off permanently, we can hunt for them using your suggestion," John said.

"I want to help in any way I can." This could be a way for her to contribute to the community.

"How are you with engines?" Mason asked, catching Sarah off guard.

Sarah was confused by the question but answered honestly. "Machines are all based on the same principles, individual parts working in unison to perform a task. Whether those parts are made of metal, wire, rubber, and so on, engines shouldn't be a problem for me." That may be oversimplified, but it was factually correct.

"I realize you're beginning to find your way among us and your new living situation, and I hate even asking. However, I don't want to pull Ben off what he's doing," Riker explained.

"What is it you want from me?" Sarah asked, cutting to the chase.

"We don't want anything from you in the same way as your captors, but I was hoping I could convince you to look at one of the tractors down on the field level," Axel continued. "Jack and Trek have been having one hell of a time keeping it running smoothly."

"The tractor is important to our sustainability while we're underground," Raz explained. "We need to make sure we have enough food for everyone here and those we rescue."

Sarah looked at Joseph once again in question. "This is totally up to you, sweetheart," he said.

She had noticed he'd begun calling her the endearment on occasion, and she liked it.

"Let me see if I understand. You want me to fix the tractor engine?" Sarah had learned it was always best to clarify.

"If you want to and if you can," Mason said. "We would never force you to do anything."

Excitement coursed through her veins. "I want to be useful and contribute to my new pack, clan… Uh, family."

She hadn't meant to say family, but this was the closest she'd been to having one in decades. The term must have gone over well by the smiles on the leaders' faces.

"We are in your debt. If there is any way you can help keep this place running to feed and shelter all of us, it would take a huge worry off our shoulders," Mason said.

"I will help keep the mechanics of this place safe and working properly." She had a purpose. An honest and helpful purpose. "Thank you for allowing me to find my place."

"You ever need anything, go to one of your new friends or come to us," Raz said with a smile.

That's right. Now she had friends.

"I hate to push this, but is there any way Joseph could take you there to have a look at the engine now?" Mason asked. "The tractor has been down for three days."

"Of course." She could start contributing right away.

"On behalf of all of us, thank you," Axel stated while opening his arms to indicate the entire table.

Sarah wasn't quite sure what to say. The leaders were thanking her as if she were their equal. "You're welcome."

Joseph stood, and Sarah followed, releasing Zahra's hand. "Thank you for your support, Zahra." The woman had been unendingly kind to her.

"Anytime." Zahra smiled in a mischievous way.

Sarah almost bounced out of the room with happiness. There was a chance, no matter how slim, of her seeing her sister again, and along with that, she had a way of contributing, a purpose she would enjoy.

Things couldn't possibly get better than this.

Chapter Eight

Sarah looked at the massive engine in dismay. *Maybe better was a bit of an overstatement.*

"Oh, come on. You got this," Joseph, her perpetual cheerleader, reassured her.

"I have never taken a tractor engine apart before. It's larger than I thought it would be."

Joseph squeezed her shoulders. "Do the best you can. No one can ask for more than that."

The engine in question sat on top of a wood pallet on the floor in the tools room. By the looks of it, there should be nothing wrong. It shined like brand new.

"I don't know what to tell you, but we've been over it multiple times and can't seem to find the problem," Jack said. "It had been working fine, maybe better than fine, before it up and quit. We'd be grateful if you gave it a try; the corn needs to be planted, and the other tractor is busy harvesting wheat."

"I'll give it a shot." That's all she could promise.

Sarah walked over to the problem engine and laid her hand on it. Instantly the machine rose off the floor, making her a bit more at ease. She concentrated on all the inner workings. Every last screw and gasket became clear in her mind until she felt confident she could pull it apart safely.

Tapping her index finger on the cold metal as she'd done with Ben's machine, the complicated engine burst outward and hovered as individual pieces. At a gasp, Sarah turned to find a couple of wolf-shifters standing off to the side.

Before she had a chance to get nervous and lose focus on the engine, one of them said, "That's so cool."

Was it cool?

"Watch out. You might be starting your fan club," Joseph teased, making her blush.

"Stop. I'm nobody," she replied.

Joseph's face turned serious as his brows drew together. "You are not a nobody. You're everything to me."

Sarah almost lost control of the engine parts, which would have sent them crashing onto the concrete floor. Luckily, Jack and Trek's conversation helped clear her thoughts and renewed her concentration.

"Hmmm, look here, Trek. Have you ever seen this kind of build-up before?" Jack asked as he moved between the floating parts, wiping some sort of residue off several smaller pieces buried deep inside the engine.

"Can't say that I have. And it's a small amount at that," Trek answered as he wiped a bit of it onto his finger and rolled it against the pad of his thumb. He raised the liquid to smell it and curled his nose in disgust. "It smells sharp, like turpentine."

"Like antiseptic even," Jack agreed as he did the same. "Why would that be inside our gas engine?"

"We've made sure there are no chemicals on the farm level to keep the animals and crops safe," Trek said. "There's no way we could have missed that."

"Sarah, would you please set the parts down so that they can be cleaned?" Jack asked as he carefully examined the parts.

She hesitated, unsure of how to proceed. They'd asked her to place the pieces on the floor, but she could be so much more helpful.

"What's wrong?" Joseph asked as he wrapped his arm around her waist from behind, lending her his support.

"I can put it down, but wouldn't you rather I fix it first?" she asked, hoping that she wasn't overstepping her bounds.

Both Jack and Trek looked at one another and then back at her. "You can do that?"

"If you will find it useful, yes." She didn't want to tell them what to do. The only reason she'd left Ben's machine in pieces was that he wanted to learn the inner workings.

The men moved back out of the way before Trek said, "We'd find that extremely useful. We could get back to planting right away."

That would help the community, so Sarah nodded and began to concentrate on the individual parts, especially those covered in the filmy residue. She commanded the liquid to fall to the floor, and piece by piece, the parts shed the film before repairing themselves from the damage the strange liquid had caused to the inner workings. When Sarah was satisfied she'd gotten it off and the affected parts fixed, she went about reattaching the separate elements until the completed engine hovered before her once again.

"Amazing," Jack said. "There's no other way to describe what you just did."

"Yes, she is amazing," Joseph chimed in with all due seriousness.

"You can set it down now, please," Trek said.

"We'll have to check the tank and fuel lines, and clean them out if necessary, but I still don't know what it is," Jack said as he collected a bit of the residue onto a plate.

"Maybe we could have Jewel analyze it," Trek suggested.

Sarah was becoming a bit tired from the exertion and leaned back against Joseph. That had been the first time she'd used her abilities and felt good about it. Helping Ben had been risky, but she was glad she did it.

"If that's everything, I believe it's time for Sarah to rest," Joseph announced.

"Of course," Jack said. "Thank you so much for all your help. You have no idea how much time this has saved us.

"I'm happy to help where I can," she replied.

Joseph took hold of her hand and led her out of the tools room. Her day had gotten so much brighter even though she was ready for a long nap.

***

It'd been a week since Sarah had repaired the tractor engine, and she'd already been asked to have a look at a few more machines around the bunker system. Joseph had watched her flourish as the need for her assistance grew, and that was the part that worried him.

Not Sarah flourishing, but the fact that so many systems seemed to be breaking down in a relatively short time. This place had been designed to last for centuries, if not longer, so these occurrences were concerning.

Sarah rolled over in her sleep and pressed her back to his chest. Since the day Raine had her meltdown, he and Sarah had been sleeping together in the bedroom. He certainly didn't mind the new arrangement and thoroughly enjoyed wrapping his arms around her at night.

If it was comfort Sarah needed, then that's what he'd provide, no questions asked.

"But what if I wanted more?" Sarah's sleepy voice startled him as she turned back over to face him.

"Did I wake you?" Joseph asked. Ready to kick his own butt if he had ruined her much-needed rest.

"No, I usually don't sleep long, only a couple hours here or there."

Joseph had noticed that now that they slept together, and was worried that something was causing her pain or worry. "Is there anything wrong?"

"No. It's a habit I'm trying to break," she explained. "I learned to stay alert. Sleep was a luxury. Anyone could attack if you dozed off."

It broke Joseph's heart to hear her talk about the cruelty she'd endured, but he found solace in the fact that he would ensure nothing remotely similar would ever happen again.

When Sarah's question finally registered, Joseph wasn't entirely sure he'd heard her right or imagined them.

"I meant them," Sarah confirmed. "I want more."

"You're getting better at reading my thoughts every day, sweetheart."

"Good thing, too," she grumbled. "Or I would have never known how you felt about me."

"I didn't want to rush you. You've been through so much already."

"I'm the best person to decide when I'm feeling rushed," Sarah stated. "Tell me in your own words how you feel."

Talk about being put on the spot, but he wasn't a man to shy away from what he wanted. Joseph hoped he could articulate how he felt properly. He wasn't a man known for his words. He was an Enforcer, not a poet.

Sarah raised her hand and settled her palm against his jaw, calming him.

"I love you," he blurted out. "Shit, no, I didn't mean to start there."

"You don't love me?" Sarah's brows scrunched together.

"No. Yes, shit. This isn't going well, is it?" Why was he acting like an imbecile?

Sarah did the one thing that he hadn't expected at his weak attempt at a romantic gesture: she leaned forward and kissed him. It was quick, but her soft lips left a lasting impression on him.

"What was that for?" Joseph asked.

"You looked like you needed a lifeline," Sarah teased.

"If you ever feel that way again, by all means, go ahead and kiss me," Joseph said. "But I want you to know that over the many months we've been together, I've fallen in love with you. Your strength, and the kindness you've shown others…you amaze me. You greet every day with new hopes and work as hard as you can to help those around you. You've faced things head-on, fearlessly giving your all to everything you touch. I respect you. I admire you, and yes, I love you. Completely."

Sarah's silence was deafening. He finally understood that pin-dropping phrase.

His anxiety got the best of him, no matter how hard he pushed for calm. "If you don't f—"

Sarah moved her palm from his jaw to over his mouth. "I love you too, Joseph."

Joseph's heart skipped a beat and then ramped up into overdrive. She loved him. "You do?"

"How could I not?" Sarah asked. "You're perfect."

"I'm far from perfect." Joseph didn't want to lead her on to think that.

"I'll get more specific. You're perfect for me. Everything about you attracts me. Your conviction and strength, as well as your soft side."

"I'm not soft," Joseph grumbled as he puffed out his chest, which Sarah promptly slapped.

"You're soft in the ways that matter." She laughed. "The ways that count to me. You're protective, but you never stand in my way from trying something new or choosing what I wish to do with my ability. I'm free to do what I want, feel how I feel, and love who I love, and that's you. I may not have experienced a lot of the world over the past twenty years, but I do know my mind. Those emotions are mine, and I want to embrace them and welcome that love into my world."

Joseph couldn't resist running his fingers through her pure white hair before cupping the back of her head. "May I kiss you?"

"By all means," Sarah parroted his previous response with a smile.

He didn't need any further confirmation. They loved each other, and Joseph swore he'd spend his life making Sarah happy.

When their lips met this time, they weren't hurried. Sarah's soft lips parted to let him in as he explored her hot, wet mouth. Joseph wanted to taste every inch of Sarah and commit every nuance to memory. He didn't want to forget a single moment, and swore he never would.

She tasted of strawberries, a late-night treat they'd shared before bed. Their tongues dueled as their hands roamed. The feel of her warm palms exploring his chest and abdomen sent electricity through his body.

Joseph wouldn't be making love to Sarah tonight. They'd just admitted that they loved one another. It would take time for that to settle in. However, sharing that love in other ways was going to happen since he couldn't keep his hands off her soft pale skin.

As his palms ghosted over her camisole and shorts, he worried his calluses would pull on the thin fabric and ruin it.

"I'd rather feel your hands on my skin without the clothing," Sarah murmured, and Joseph took the hint and was in the process of reaching for the buttons the moment the last word left her mouth. Holding her skin to skin sounded like heaven.

Joseph was inches away from Sarah's top button when someone began pounding on their front door. That someone was going to die this evening.

Sarah's soft moan of defeat didn't help matters. "Who do you think it is this late?"

"Only one way to find out. You wait here," Joseph said before rolling out of bed and readjusting himself inside his boxer briefs. There was no way to hide what they'd been doing, and he damn well didn't care.

Joseph unlocked the door and pulled it open, revealing a grim-faced alpha. "Mason, what is it?"

"We need your help," Mason stated, and at the click of the door behind him, he knew Sarah was listening as well. "Both the air ventilation and filtration systems have gone offline. If we don't get them back up and running, the entire complex could be without clean air by ten tomorrow morning."

"Shit, we'll get dressed and be right out," Joseph said before walking back to Sarah and their bedroom.

"Has something else broken?" Sarah asked as he entered, looking as nervous as Joseph felt.

"Yes, the ventilation system this time." *What the hell is going on around here?*

"I wonder why so many things seem to be having issues lately. Was it always like this before I came here?" Sarah asked while digging through her dresser drawer.

"No. These are recent events, and they're beginning to worry me," Joseph admitted as they both pulled on their jeans.

"From what you've told me, there are many new shifters who were rescued among the original community. Could the damage be intentional?"

"That's what we're going to find out, sweetheart."

Chapter Nine

Sarah followed Alpha Mason and Joseph up through the facility to one of the upper levels. She'd never been this far away from the living quarters below. There were multiple vehicles on this level, and platforms that she imagined lifted them to the surface when needed.

This was the industrial portion of the facility. Metal beams and walls, all painted gray, covered the area while machines completing different functions rumbled and hummed a symphony around her.

Various shifters were working in the vast stadium-like area, and Sarah felt like she was getting a behind-the-scenes tour of how the bunkers remained inhabitable.

"It's over here," Mason said while pointing at what Sarah hoped wasn't the machine they needed her to fix.

When they stopped in front of it, she couldn't help but gasp. This wasn't going to be easy. Sarah felt like an ant standing beside something that reminded her of a turbine encased in a giant half-circle of steel several stories high.

Many people stood on the inside and outside of the machine. Lights had been set up to illuminate the darker spaces and crevices of the internal workings. Piles of metal sheets used to cover critical components lay removed and off to the side, revealing what looked like large metal shavings the size of her wrist. Whatever had happened inside the casing of the machine caused a significant amount of damage to the entire structure.

Mason led them through the group of shifters gathered, and up to the base of the machine where Axel, Xander, Riker, and John stood waiting. Axel was holding a mangled bit of steel that bore a resemblance to a tool of some kind.

"What have you found?" Mason asked as they joined them.

Sarah was holding on to Joseph like a lifeline. There were many shifters around them, and she was still a hyena after all.

"They'd have to get through me, the alphas, betas, and John to get anywhere near you," Joseph assured while pulling her closer to his side.

"This," Axel answered as he held out the piece of metal. "Rudimentary, but it did the job nicely."

"What was it?" John asked.

"My best guess, a ratchet," Axel answered.

"That's a big ratchet," Sarah said. Her father had many tools but nothing as impressive as that, even if it was broken.

"We have to maintain quite a few large pieces of machinery," Joseph explained. "They require large tools to do the job."

"How'd that get in there?" Mason asked while running the palm of his hand down his face.

"I believe we all know what's been going on around here lately," Axel stated. "We have a saboteur. A traitor amongst us."

Sarah's anxiety skyrocketed, but when she glanced around, no one was looking at her. Right, she wasn't considered a traitor anymore.

Someone was going about intentionally trying to destroy vital machinery all across the facility if her recent string of repairs were anything to go by. Who would want to do something so heinous to their fellow shifters and survivors?

When the leaders turned to look at Sarah, she knew what was coming next.

"Do you think you could have a look at it, Sarah? Maybe give us a direction to go in fixing it?" Xander asked.

"You don't wish me to fix it?" That made more people turn and stare, not what she'd intended to do.

"We thought that perhaps this might be harder on you than the other machines, and there's no way we'd ask you to harm yourself," Riker explained.

"First, let me take a look around inside," Sarah said. "Then, I can give you a better idea of how much I can do." She didn't want to commit before seeing the extent of the damage up close.

"Perfect," Mason said. "Thank you."

Joseph led her over to the machine and had her wait until he'd checked the way in for any hidden dangers. It didn't matter to him that other workers were already inside, he rechecked the sharp bits, bending them out of the way, and no one said a word.

"Okay, sweetheart, give me your hand," Joseph said as he reached down for her. "I'm happy you wore a decent pair of shoes for this."

"Me too," Sarah agreed. There were metal bits everywhere. She never professed to know how all machines work, but her gift gave her the ability to break machines down into their basic parts and repair any damage from the inside out by influencing the metal.

Workers stepped out of her way, allowing her to move deeper into the cavernous machine. "Seriously, how did they get this in here?"

"Piece by piece, over the years," Joseph answered.

"Wow," Sarah said as the area opened up into what looked to be holding three giant fan blades. A large metal pin spanning at least twenty feet held them in place.

She imagined it took a lot of power to circulate the air through so many levels. There were other components to the left, but something was calling her to the right. Joseph stayed right by her side as she began placing her palms on different sections of metal.

Sarah sorted through the vibrations coming from the other machines in the room and concentrated on what appeared to be the most heavily damaged area.

"This way," she said before moving farther into the right side of the metal goliath.

If the damage was located to only one half of the machine, Sarah had a chance to fix it. She stopped in a section that appeared to have nothing salvageable left. Metal, twisted and torn away, revealed a giant hole where a metal shaft used to be attached.

"I need to get this outside cover off." She tapped the hunk of metal in front of her. "Then, we shall see."

Joseph took hold of her hands. "Are you sure this won't be too much for you? I swore I'd keep you safe even if it's from yourself."

Sarah couldn't help but love the big guy. "I love you, Joseph."

"I love you, too, but that doesn't answer my question." Persistent.

Sarah took a deep breath and said, "I believe I can help. It would take a serious amount of shifter hours to fix this, and I honestly think there's not enough time for that. The airflow has stopped, meaning no fresh air for anyone in the bunkers. I have to try."

Joseph gathered her into his arms and held her tight. "And you keep trying to tell me you're not fearless."

"Oh, there's plenty of fear, but there's also so much to lose if I allow it to rule me as it has in my past," Sarah explained.

Joseph released his hold on her and began leading her back out. There were a few more people present now than when they'd left, making her uneasy. Did they come to see the freak perform? Sarah spun her bracelet around her wrist, trying to use up some of her nervous energy.

Once they were out, Joseph took the lead. "We need all unnecessary personnel to leave before Sarah begins. There are too many people for her to be comfortable."

"Of course," Mason answered. "You think you can do it, Sarah?"

She didn't want to lie or give false hope. "I feel better about it since having a look inside. I will try as hard as I can."

The two betas, Xander and Riker, along with John, began dispersing the crowds, leaving only the workers there to help fix the gigantic machine. She walked over to the right side of the beast and placed her palms against the metal once again, but from the outside, confirming this was the best point of entry.

A four-inch metal plate covering the entire right side was bolted into the main structure. She should be able to remove it without too much of a bother. While she walked around the end of the machine, she overheard a few shifters talking about how they'd never thought they'd see the day.

Sarah didn't need to hear the entire conversation to know they were talking about her, a hyena, helping them of all things. A loud growl had them quieting as Joseph joined her.

"Easy, big guy, we might need their help once I get this baby cracked open."

Joseph pulled her close and kissed her softly, as if declaring their bond for all to see.

"You ready to give this a try, sweetheart?" Joseph asked, his facial features schooled in an attempt to hide his concern.

"Let's do this," she said while shaking out her hands. "I'll need a large area cleared so I can set this end piece down once I've detached it."

He nodded, gave her another quick kiss, and headed back to the alphas. Sarah placed herself at the center point of the piece of steel she intended to move. With one final look around to make sure everyone had gotten out of the way, she began.

Placing both palms against the cold surface, she allowed her power to flow through her once again. Sarah was careful to limit it to only the piece she wanted to be removed and began mentally unscrewing the many bolts holding it to the central hub of the machine.

Sarah commanded the metal plate to detach before she began lifting it into the air. A murmur of voices didn't bother her; she understood it wasn't every day someone who barely broke five foot five raised a couple of tons of steel.

She moved back away from the plate while retaining control over it. Then slowly inch by inch, she pulled the cover off and moved it onto an open space on the floor. A few claps sounded when she released her hold on the metal, and it settled gently on the cement.

Of course, she blushed. She always blushed. Sarah wished she had some way to control it, but with her pale skin, it was impossible.

"Never change, your rosy cheeks are beautiful," Joseph said as he joined her once again.

"Thank you." She laughed, feeling infinitely better. "Now, let's have a look inside from this new perspective."

The others were gathered around but parted to let her pass. When Sarah saw the extent of the damage, she made sure to calm her features. This repair was going to take a bit more then she'd expected.

A large section looked like a bomb had gone off inside it. Jagged pieces of metal stabbed out in all directions while other parts dangled limply, reminding her of cooked spaghetti. This wasn't good.

A tall man with hair the coloring of a Bengal tiger said as he raked his hand over his face, "Whoever is responsible for this did their job well. I don't think we'd be able to repair it in time to evacuate the bunkers."

"That's Matriarch Raz's father, Gareth," Joseph answered her unasked question.

Sarah had found it fascinating that a tiger Matriarch ruled over wolf-shifters, while a wolf Matriarch ruled over a clan of bear-shifters. If that didn't say inclusion, Sarah didn't know what did.

There were badgers, moles, tigers, lions, birds of prey, bears, wolves, fox, and many more among them, all within this facility. Maybe a hyena could find her place here as well.

The word "evacuate" seemed amplified in her head as the thought of leaving the only place she'd had to call home was terrifying and a definite no-go.

"I'll try to fix it," Sarah blurted out.

They all stopped talking. Shit.

"Can you do that, sweetheart," Joseph asked, "without hurting yourself?"

"We'd all be in a lot more danger if we have to leave this place. Allow me the chance to repair it while you continue with your evacuation plans." Gods knew she didn't want them to bet everything on her pulling this off.

Mason and Axel exchanged glances, obviously discussing the merits of her idea. They were responsible for many shifters' lives. Sarah understood that and would respect their decision.

Finally, Mason looked at her. "We'll give you a chance to fix it. How many people do you need to help?"

"Only a handful in case I have questions or need assistance." There wouldn't be much else they could do while she was working on the machine.

"Okay, the rest of you will help with the evacuation," Axel ordered. "Move out. There's a lot to be done in a short period of time."

Sarah couldn't help but ask, "Where will we go?"

Joseph held her close. "There is a second location, but it's over one hundred miles away and not as well prepared as here. We'd begun construction on it a decade ago in case something happened to this location. We should've started sooner."

Sarah watched the fear light in the other shifters' faces. She was familiar with that look as she'd often worn it herself.

Taking a deep breath, Sarah pulled herself together and said, "Let's begin."

Chapter Ten

"She can't fix what I've done," he hissed.

"I wouldn't be so sure," Rachel growled. "This hyena has proven herself to be a thorn in my side from the beginning." She remembered how close she was to turning that young Enforcer until that dinner. Who could blame her for being hostile when faced with a dirty hyena?

"What do we do?" her accomplice asked. It had proved to be exceptionally difficult finding decent help in the bunkers.

"I don't mind getting hyena blood on my hands. Do you?" she asked with a biting laugh while extending her claws from her fingertips. "My precious falcon."

"It would be a pleasure to assist you, but how?" he asked. "That big wolf is always with her. There's no way he'd let me near her."

"We'll have to figure out a way to separate them," Rachel said as she contemplated her options. "We'll get her alone and deal with her my way. Nothing is going to keep me locked up underground here with these heathen shifters, even if I have to claw my way to the surface."

"Except me, right?" he whined. Rachel couldn't wait to drop the poultry as soon as she could.

She looked at the falcon shifter and smiled coyly. "Of course not. You're a majestic falcon fit to stand by my side. We will find a place more suited to our needs. Perhaps one of my family's homes in the California hills where we can start over."

"Yes, California. Sun and surfing." He almost salivated, disgusting Rachel even further.

"Of course, dear, anything you want." She laid it on thick, and the bird-brain bought it all. "However, first, we must do away with the hyena. She stands in the way of us getting to the surface and beginning our new life together."

His eyes turned dark, and he began to grin. "Your wish is my command."

***

Joseph, along with the others who remained with Sarah, were busy collecting the broken pieces of metal scattered across the floor. Sarah would need them all in order to return the ventilation system to its original form.

A door slammed shut, causing him to turn and check on the identity of their new arrival. Sarah didn't need any bullshit biases from anyone right now. The new guy rushed over to Gareth, looking a bit flustered with his eyes darting around the area.

"Where have you been, Severn?" Gareth demanded. "You were called thirty minutes ago."

"Sorry, sir, got sidetracked," Severn said by way of explanation. A pretty shoddy one at that.

Gareth shook his head at the man before pointing in Joseph's direction. "If you weren't an engineer, I'd toss you out on your ass. Help them pick up all the loose pieces."

Severn nodded and began walking over but not before taking an unmistakable side glance at Sarah, who was standing by the machine.

"You have a problem?" Joseph asked when the man drew near.

"No. Curious about the hyena, that's all," he replied.

"Her name is Sarah," Joseph growled. "Understand?"

Sarah didn't need another person making her feel out of place no matter what this guy's deal was. It would take time for her to be accepted, but now wasn't the time to coddle anyone who was still undecided.

"I meant no harm," Severn said while holding his hands up in front of himself in surrender. "I haven't met her yet, that's all."

"Now's not the time for introductions," Joseph warned before pointing to a box of metal pieces. "Start collecting those."

Severn immediately picked up the box and walked several feet away. The guy didn't give Joseph a calm feeling, which usually meant trouble, and as an Enforcer, he went with his gut instincts.

Once Joseph had filled a second box, he brought both over to Sarah, where she and Gareth stood holding on to a diagram.

"So that's what it's meant to look like," Sarah said as she held up a small piece of shredded metal, and right before his eyes, the metal warped and transformed itself to resemble the part in the picture.

"How's it going here?" Joseph asked as he set the boxes down and wrapped his arm around Sarah's waist. She was under a tremendous amount of stress, and he wanted to lend his strength to her whenever he could.

The piece that had reassembled itself floated from her hand and back into the machine before Sarah answered. "Slowly. I need to come up with a way to repair larger sections at once, or I'll never have enough time before the evacuation must begin."

"There might be a way," Gareth said. "There were blueprints showing larger sections of the interior."

"Great, let's get them," Sarah stated.

Gareth didn't look as happy as Sarah sounded. "Well, the thing is, I'm not entirely sure where they are."

"You don't have them backed up on one of the many computers around here?" Joseph asked in shock.

"With everything going on, there hasn't been enough time. Remember when this machine began being built, not only weren't computers in every household, they weren't even invented yet and we still communicated by the telegraph. It wasn't uncommon for a lot of information to be stored in paper files," Gareth explained.

"Where do we look?" Sarah asked. "Maybe we can find it." Joseph had noticed Sarah's optimistic outlook shining through on a more frequent basis in the past few weeks.

"They should be in the file room one level down, but again I'm not sure where in the walls of cabinets those drawings are located," Gareth explained. "It's a needle in a haystack kind of search."

"Then we'll take the remaining men and tear the place apart if we have to," Joseph stated as he began calling more shifters over, including Severn; there was no way he'd leave the shifty-eyed guy here with Sarah. "We need everyone's help to find a specific blueprint that will make the repairs move more quickly."

"I'll take you to the room," Gareth said and began walking away.

Joseph looked down at Sarah. "Are you going to be okay up here without me?"

"Of course, everyone else is too busy preparing to evacuate even to notice me. Besides, we need those drawings. If I can put multiple pieces back together at the same time, we'd at least have a chance."

Joseph leaned down and kissed his soon-to-be mate. Their mating was going to happen after this crisis was averted. He desperately wanted to begin this new chapter of his life with the woman he loved and cherished more than anyone or anything in this entire world.

"So positive of yourself, are you?" Sarah teased, and Joseph could feel his face flush. "Go find my blueprints; then we'll talk about mating."

He couldn't contain his smile at her playful grin, so Joseph stole another kiss and ran after the others. He'd find those blueprints, they'd fix the machine, and their community would be safe again.

When he caught up to Gareth, they were already descending the staircase leading to the next level. The room Gareth had led them to wasn't too far down the brightly lit hallway, but when he opened the door, Joseph finally understood what the tiger had meant by walls of files. Filing cabinets stood in every direction Joseph could see— some had five drawers, others six.

"Seriously," Joseph groaned.

"I'm afraid so," Gareth answered.

"Okay, let's get to work and hope our shifter speed helps us find the blueprints before it's too late," Joseph instructed as he took hold of the first filing cabinet he came to. "Anything you find that includes a drawing show it to Gareth, he's the only one who knows what we're looking for."

If they survived this, he was going to make sure to ask their leaders to assign a full-time person to scan all of the older information into the computer system so that this would never happen again.

When he reached his fifth cabinet, Joseph took a second to look around at the others' progress. Immediately, he noticed one shifter missing: Severn. *"Fuck."*

***

Sarah flipped through the stack of drawings she'd already been given, hoping for more detailed pictures, but found none. Usually, she'd allow the parts to repair themselves all at once, but the machine was so big she wasn't sure she had the strength to do it. If she tried one massive fix and ended up passing out, all would be lost, so until they found the other more complete diagrams, she worked on one piece at a time.

Joseph and the others had been gone for a long time. Sarah was beginning to worry they might not find what she needed when one of the shifters who'd been working with Joseph appeared through a doorway.

"Have they found it?' Sarah asked as the man drew nearer.

"They've found a few things, but they're not sure that it's exactly what you need. Gareth has asked me to come and get you so you could go down to the file room and take a look at them," he explained. "It would be a lot easier than hauling them all up here to find out they're not the ones you require."

Sarah felt unsure of whether she wanted to follow this shifter anywhere. His eyes were constantly scanning their surroundings, and the nervous energy radiating off him was concerning. Then again, she understood his responses could be due to the dire situation they found themselves in.

When Sarah took too long to answer, he continued. "I knew it. You don't want to help other shifters, not really. You can't even be bothered to come down one flight of stairs to check out the drawings we found. As sure as shit, you've got everyone fooled."

"No. No, I'll come and take a look. I want to help." Sarah didn't want to cause any trouble, and she certainly didn't want anyone to question her loyalty in a time like this.

They'd walked through the side door when she was violently pulled aside and had a rag cover her nose and mouth. A sharp pain tore through the back of her head, then darkness and nothing more.

***

"You kill her," a female said, and Sarah recognized that voice. Rachel.

Instead of moving, Sarah lay absolutely still. Whatever they'd hit her with, it wasn't hard enough to cause any lasting damage to a hyena shifter. She'd woken up in what looked like a large storeroom or warehouse, but the shelves were empty, and she couldn't help but wonder if the stock had already been moved to the other site.

Sarah wasn't sure how long she'd been out, but any time away from the ventilation system would be disastrous. She had to figure out a way to get out of here.

She tried their link. *"Joseph."*

"Sarah, where are you?" Joseph's panic-stricken voice came in loud and clear.

"In a stockroom of some kind, it's empty, though." That was all she could see from her position lying on the floor while the other two continued to argue behind her.

"Who's with you?"

"Severn and Rachel." She'd known there was something wrong with that lioness.

"Are you hurt?" His worry was a living thing.

"Only a headache from where they hit me."

"I will end them," Joseph growled.

"Could you make it soon because they're trying to decide who's going to kill me."

Anger, sharp and deadly, whipped through the link. *"I'm on my way, sweetheart."*

"I don't want to get my claws dirty. You go ahead and do this for me, and I'll give you anything you want," Rachel spoke suggestively.

It didn't take a scientist to figure out what Rachel was offering Severn, and Sarah knew the idiot was going to fall for it.

"Anything I want?" Severn asked.

Yep, hook, line, and sinker. The shifter was a sucker.

"Anything," Rachel purred. "All you have to do is this one teensy, tiny job for me, and I'd be exceedingly grateful."

The moment Sarah heard footsteps nearing her, she jumped to her feet, shifted into her hyena, and tore off in the opposite direction away from her would-be murderers. It wasn't long before she heard claws scraping on the concrete floor behind her. Sarah was surprised that she could only hear the one beast following behind her until a piercing scream announced a falcon diving at her from above.

Sarah had been so preoccupied with worry that she didn't even realize Severn was a bird. That only meant one thing: the claws behind her were that of a lioness. Hyenas and lions did not mix. Any nature show would provide all the proof you'd need. Sarah sprinted as fast as she could around the racks, searching for a way out.

Rachel would have the advantage of her size and strength, but Sarah had cunning. When she came to the end of another long row, she turned around to face Rachel head-on.

Here kitty, kitty.

Severn dove at Sarah once again using his sharp talons to tear at her skin as he flew past, and though she was bleeding now, she didn't move. When Rachel came around the corner, her golden eyes zeroed in on Sarah.

The next time Severn dove past her, Sarah summoned the metal panel covering an emergency light to detach and used it to knock the bird out of the air. One down for now, on to the bitch.

Sarah felt like she was in some sort of western standoff. Her on the one end, Rachel on the other, when the lioness did something completely unexpected: she shifted back into a human.

"You have nowhere to go, hyena, accept your fate," Rachel stated with a toothy smile.

Sarah didn't even bother shifting to respond, knowing that was what Rachel wanted—she was killing time until her feathered accomplice came to and attacked her again.

"You're ruining my chances of getting out of the bunkers," the lioness accused, "and back home."

Rachel wanted to leave the facility protecting her?

"All it was going to take was for a few systems to break, and then they'd be ferrying us to the surface and my freedom. However, you decided to fix them."

Why would anyone want to go outside? It was crazy out there right now; with Collectors, hunters, and hyenas on the move no one was safe.

"You see, I wasn't made to live like this. My family has many homes around the world, and I intend to return to one of them."

Okay, she was straight-up crazy. There was nothing left to go back to. Maybe Sarah could reason with her, so she gave in and shifted.

"Nothing is remaining of your homes and your family. Don't you see that? If you leave here, you'd be either caught or dead by the end of the day." Sarah went with the blunt truth, hoping to get through to Rachel.

"What does a hyena know? Nothing." Rachel sneered. "Your entire species excels at lying and cheating."

Sarah had given it a shot and prudently shifted back into her stronger hyena as Rachel shifted as well. The lioness dug her four-inch claws into the concrete floor, chipping out pieces as she went. She jumped forward, charging straight at Sarah, leaving her with no other choice.

Sarah commanded the solid steel racks to twist and fall in front of Rachel, blocking her path. The lioness roared her anger and clawed at the steel. Sarah backed up farther away from the crumpled metal, bumping into a wall as she did.

Before Sarah had a chance to run, the lioness broke free of the bent metal and lunged, claws out, for Sarah's throat. Then a blur flashed between them, and Rachel was gone, confusing Sarah until she heard the fight carrying on to the left of her.

Joseph, in his magnificent silver wolf form, was taking on the lioness, exchanging blow for blow. Sarah looked over at the others gathered, wondering why they weren't helping Joseph.

"Miss, there is no way I'd get between Joseph and his right to protect you as your intended mate," Gareth answered her unasked question. "Don't worry. Joseph is an Enforcer for a reason."

When Sarah turned back, Joseph had Rachel's lioness pinned to the floor, his sharp teeth inches from her neck.

"Joseph, I'm safe. You don't have to end her."

"She intended to kill you." His wolf was in complete control, defending his mate at all costs.

"That's what makes us different from her, our innate sense of right and wrong, mate."

Joseph clamped down on the lioness's throat but didn't break the skin. Though his intentions were clear, he released her and stepped back closer to Sarah.

The place lit up after that. Raz and Zahra appeared before them with their mates. "I apologize we're late, but we were teleporting provisions to the second site," Mason said as he stepped toward Rachel. "Shift." Rachel did so immediately, for once realizing she had no other choice.

Sarah didn't care what happened to Rachel and Severn; she needed to get back to fixing the machine. She shifted, and so did

Joseph, who took Gareth's offered jacket to wrap it around Sarah's body.

"I have to get back to the machine; we're running out of time."

At Joseph's grim expression, her stomach turned. "We're out of time. The community is making its way up as we speak."

"No," Sarah said. How long was she knocked out? "Please, take me there." She would not give up until she was too weak to continue. "This place is too important not to give me a chance, please."

Joseph pulled her closer as someone threw him a pair of shorts.

"I'm sorry, Sarah," Gareth said, and the more she knew about Raz's father, the more she understood his decency and nature. "We can't risk leaving it too late and someone being hurt."

She looked up at Joseph. *"I need you to believe in me."* Sarah knew it was a lot to ask in this type of unpredictable and possibly catastrophic situation.

Joseph didn't look away. Instead, he smiled. "I believe in you. You'll have your chance, sweetheart."

Things moved quickly after that. Somehow, Raz waved her hand, and Sarah was clothed once again, making her wonder why the goddesses didn't take a crack at the machine.

"That is a logical question, Sarah," Raz answered, shocking Sarah until she remembered Raz was a mage and could hear her thoughts. "We may be goddesses, but our power isn't infinite. We need to make sure and use it to move every person and possession from this location to the second one. If we were to tire out, after unsuccessfully attempting to repair the ventilation system, our people would be stranded here without clean air."

"Let's go, time is of the essence," Mason ordered, and those returning to the machine joined hands, while the others remained to take Rachel and Severn into custody.

The storeroom vanished.

Chapter Eleven

When they returned to the machine, the surroundings looked different from when she'd left before the attack. Shifters were gathering in groups and preparing to be teleported away from their homes yet again. Joseph had told her how hard it had been to leave everything they knew the first time; even their possessions going back centuries were left behind as they raced to safety. The sense of loss must have been crushing.

The shifters gathered were far enough back as to not get in her way as she approached the metal beast. The time for small repairs was over. She'd either repair the ventilation system or doom hundreds of shifters to suffer another move to a site not so homey and comfortable as this one.

"Are you sure about this, sweetheart?" Joseph asked as he stood behind her, ever her rock. "I'll stand by your side through whatever comes."

Sarah looked back across the expanse at the visibly upset and terrified shifters clutching what few belongings they could carry. She noticed Marie and Ben. Beside them stood Hope, Jenny, Matthew, and Archie, their dog. Hope's red-rimmed eyes matched those of the children, but Sarah could tell she was holding it together for them. Gone were their happy faces and friendly waves. Instead, they were frightened with wide eyes and burgeoning tears.

"I need the workers to go join their families and the groups to depart," Sarah said. "They can no longer assist me. Except for Gareth. I would like to speak with him before he leaves."

"You've got it," Joseph said and left to do as she asked. They should all be with their families at a time like this. She'd want to be if she had any left.

That sad thought had barely left her mind when Gareth joined her. "What do you need?"

Sarah had sensed Gareth was a loyal and decent shifter, that's why he'd get this critical job. "Do you have a family that needs your assistance?" She would never take him away from those he loved.

"I'm a widower, and my sons and daughter are grown and able to care for themselves. I can remain behind and help in any way I can."

Sarah believed she'd made the right choice. "I need you to do something for me. To take care of a few friends of mine because I'm not sure how this will end, and they will need someone to look out for them."

"With my life," Gareth agreed, confirming her belief of his worth.

"Them," Sarah said as she pointed out Hope and the children. "You are to protect them. Do I have your word?"

Gareth looked her straight in the eye and said, "You have my solemn oath."

Sarah placed her hand against his arm. "Thank you, Gareth. You have no idea how important that is to me."

She turned back to face her mechanical nemesis. She'd never taken on anything this big or this damaged. Well, there was a first time for everything.

***

Joseph watched as Gareth made his way over to Hope and the children. "Want to tell me what that's all about?'

"Hope needs someone to watch out for her and the children," Sarah said as if her request was reasonable.

"Hope's a bear shifter. She could take on anyone who tried to hurt her or the kids." Hell, Hope would give him a good wallop.

"Not every form of protection is strength-based. Hope holds up well, but she's lonely and alone, and has to deal with everything thrown at her."

"You're playing matchmaker in the middle of a crisis?"

"I can't tell you if they're a match or not, but at least now there's a chance to find out. I want my friend to be happy, and I may not have another opportunity."

Joseph leaned down and kissed Sarah with all the love and passion he had, only coming up when they both needed to breathe.

"You're one of a kind, and I'm here to make sure you have all the chances you need. I love you."

"I love you too," Sarah said as she ran the palm of her hand over his jaw. "Now, let's get this thing up and running again."

Once everyone had cleared away, he and Sarah stood facing the end she'd opened earlier. A row of boxes containing broken and bent parts sat on the floor in front of it.

"What do you need me to do?" Joseph asked.

"I need all those extra bits thrown back in so that the pieces are present when I try to repair it all at once."

Joseph couldn't help but worry. He shoved it down and did as she had asked. While he worked, Sarah ran her palms over the exterior, getting a feel for the work that needed to be done.

Onlookers kept their distance as more shifters gathered to be teleported away if this should fail. There was no way Joseph could shield Sarah from their curious and some hostile looks. Not everyone had had the opportunity to meet Sarah and discover how kind and gentle she was.

Once every last metal bit and shaving was thrown back inside the machine, Sarah rejoined him upfront. "It's all in there, sweetheart."

Sarah looked up at him, and Joseph knew he wasn't going to like what she was about to say. "You should join the others where it's safe."

"Not getting rid of me that easily. I'm staying right here with you."

"If it doesn't work—"

"If it doesn't work, we'll leave here together."

Sarah wrapped her arms around his waist and hugged him. "Okay, but stand behind me."

"Anywhere you say," he agreed before kissing her on the forehead and moving behind her.

"This might get a little wild, but whatever you do, don't pull me away."

"Unless you are in danger, I will not move you." That was all he could promise.

Sarah took a deep breath and blew it out before raising her hands at the machine. It was now or never.

***

The pull was instantaneous. Sarah's powers flowed from her and into the tons of steel standing before her until it felt as if it were part of her body. The damage she hadn't been able to see visually came into clear focus now, giving her pause to refine her game plan to include the additional damage.

Even though her eyes were closed, Sarah could still see the machine, but in a more multidimensional way. She searched through feet of steel for the exact point to begin. A place that would start a chain reaction of repairs cascading forward until the ventilation system performed like new. It sounded good in theory.

The machine began to shake as the metal came to life to do Sarah's bidding. She felt Joseph wrap his arms around her waist when her feet left the ground, but nothing was going to stop her. Sarah had a home here with Joseph and her friends, and she wouldn't let them down.

Sarah could feel she was getting closer when every last piece of metal in the machine came to life, and she found the tipping point. She called it that because, with one perfectly placed push, the repairs would come cascading down like dominos.

The machine was beginning to rise off its mounts. Sarah could hear gasps of shock from the people gathered, but she refused to let it distract her. Joseph's grip around her tightened as her body threatened to go skyward with the machine. With his solid reinforcement she remained close to the ground. He'd been her rock since the first time they'd laid eyes on one another.

With his solid support, she pushed even harder at its core, making the metal tremble. Then, as if it had been merely waiting for her all along, the exact spot to begin showed itself.

Sarah would have cheered if she could, but her body was otherwise occupied with keeping the metal behemoth aloft. That was where she'd begin and thus threw all her power into that one piece, transforming it back into its original shape and purpose while weaving the next section through it. She'd always likened this process to building a model, only on an industrial scale.

As the number of repaired pieces grew, so did the stress on her ability and body, but Sarah refused to rest. Instead, she pushed even more of herself into the machine in an effort to move as quickly as possible because, in the end, she doubted she'd still be conscious.

Sarah couldn't help but wonder how this whole scene appeared to the others. The metal was floating, bending, and moving in front of them, seeming almost alive. For a moment, the word freak tried to derail her, but with Joseph's immediate reassurance and love, she pushed all doubts far away.

They were almost to the halfway mark by her best estimation. Wiring snaked in and out, around the parts, reattaching themselves. Her ability allowed her to move any object as necessary, but she had an affinity for metals. Things were moving faster now as the flow of repairs steamrolled forward, picking up speed. Parts she'd never seen before repaired themselves, and those requiring more metal took from the pieces Joseph had thrown back in.

The machine rumbled and shook, but Sarah held on tight to her control over the leviathan. Her body was getting weaker, but her mind fought on, making her concentrate even harder. Soon the repairs were close to completion as the tons of steel returned to rest on its concrete moorings set into the floor.

Moments away from victory and Sarah realized they were short a couple of inches of metal. They'd missed a piece somewhere, and there was no time to find it. She looked at the bracelet Joseph had given her, heartbroken at what she was considering doing with it.

"I'll make you another, love. I promise," Joseph said above the din of metal scraping metal. "I can't think of a better way to share our love."

No sooner had the words left his mouth, and Sarah released her hold on the bracelet, allowing it to be sucked into the machine and becoming a permanent piece of the battle they'd fought to save this facility.

Her thoughts were becoming fuzzy, but she pushed forward right up until the thick steel plate she'd originally removed slid and bolted itself back into place. Once the last bolt was tightened, Sarah commanded the machine to start before she fell back into Joseph's arms.

A loud whirring noise preceded the beast rumbling to life, and the last thing she remembered was Joseph's handsome face hovering above hers.

Gods, she loved this man.

Chapter Twelve

Joseph paced around Sarah's bed. He'd brought her back to their bedroom after Jewel and the Goddesses confirmed that Sarah was unharmed and would be back to normal after getting some rest. That had been hours ago, and she still hadn't woken. Joseph was well aware he wasn't rational, that it would take time for her to gain her strength, but what he'd give to see Sarah's pale eyes open.

The ventilation system was back up and running, and thanks to Sarah, no one had to leave their homes behind for a second time. Items that had been teleported over to the other site were now returned to their original locations as if nothing had happened.

Numerous people had already stopped in to check on Sarah. Hope and the children followed by Gareth, Marie, Ben, all the leaders, and Solomon. The last visitor surprised the hell out of Joseph. He hadn't talked to his brother about the events of that dinner, and they'd seen each other only briefly when Raine went scaly, but that had been it, until now.

Solomon stood in the kitchen unwrapping food he'd brought over for Joseph and Sarah, saying she'd need her energy and Joseph couldn't cook worth a damn. In truth, Joseph had been avoiding going into the other room, not needing more drama than he had already.

"Joseph," Solomon said from behind him. "Can we talk for a moment, please?"

Obviously, avoidance wasn't going to work. "Now may be the worst possible time for you and me to have a chat." Solomon had brought that damn lioness into his and Sarah's home.

"I understand," Solomon said. "I want you to know how sorry I am."

"Fine, you want to talk, let's talk," Joseph growled as he stormed out of the bedroom. The last thing he wanted to do was disturb Sarah's much-needed rest.

"I know I was out of line," Solomon began.

"Out of line? Is that what you call accusing me of being a traitor simply because I'm with Sarah when in truth you bring the traitor, who could have gotten everyone killed, to our dinner table? Then your date insults Sarah on multiple occasions until I'm forced to kick her out of our home. Then we find out the crazy bitch is trying to kill Sarah to stop her from saving this facility we all call home."

"I—"

"I'm not done," Joseph growled deeply as his wolf pushed at him for freedom. "You forced Sarah to be degraded and humiliated in her own home without raising a finger to stop your 'date.' Tell me, why should I accept an apology from an Enforcer who couldn't see the traitor past his own dick?" Joseph's chest was heaving, and he wasn't sure it was all because of Solomon.

"Can you please make up already and stop yelling?" Sarah's voice rang out from the bedroom. "You love your brother."

Joseph took off at a run and was beside his love within seconds. "How do you feel? Does anything hurt? Do you need anything?"

Sarah opened her beautiful blue eyes, smiled at him, and answered. "Good. No. You."

Joseph couldn't help himself, he crawled onto the bed and pulled Sarah into his arms. "You had me worried, sweetheart."

"I had me worried." She laughed. "Now, make up with your brother."

"It's not that easy," Solomon said from the doorway. "What I've done is unforgivable."

"That woman had everyone fooled. Live and learn, then move on. Life is far too short even for shifters to throw family away," Sarah said as she cuddled in closer to Joseph's chest.

Joseph understood what Sarah meant. She'd had no one, and only the faint hope of finding her sister. "I can't promise anything, but we can try."

"Really?" Solomon said in what Joseph assumed was shock.

At Sarah's smile, he said, "Yes, really. Now go away."

"Happy to see you better, Sarah. We'll talk soon."

"Are you positive you're not in any pain?" Joseph asked.

"Maybe a bit stiff, but otherwise fine," Sarah replied as she rubbed the back of her neck.

"I'll run you a hot bath so you can have a good soak and loosen up those muscles," Joseph said before carefully moving Sarah aside, rolling off the bed and heading for the bathroom. Sarah's happy chuckles helped to improve his mood significantly.

***

Since she'd woken in their bedroom, Sarah presumed the repair to the ventilation system worked, but she had to be sure. "Everything is working properly?" she asked as she walked into the bathroom.

Joseph stood from the filling bathtub to grab her around the waist. "Should you be walking so soon?"

Sarah couldn't help but kiss the big worrywart. "I'm fine, honest."

"I'm going to put in Epsom salt to help relax your muscles, and yes, the machine is working. Maybe better than it ever has, thanks to you," Joseph explained.

"Thanks to us," Sarah corrected. "If you hadn't been there lending me your strength, I doubt we would have been so successful."

Before Joseph could argue further, Sarah began slipping out of her shorts and shirt, distracting the big guy from any further discussion about who did what. Unfortunately, he wasn't removing his clothing as she had hoped.

Once naked, she slid into the hot water and moaned her relief. "This feels wonderful, aren't you going to join me?"

Joseph seemed to snap out of it and said, "This is for you. I want to make you feel better."

"I'll tell you what will make me feel better, you and me in this tub."

"Are you sure?" Joseph appeared to be having some sort of internal struggle.

Sarah didn't even bother answering. She raised one eyebrow and stared him down. Her love was out of his clothing in five seconds flat. When Joseph sat down on the opposite end of the tub from her, she couldn't help but join him.

"You're too far away from me over there," she teased as her body brushed up against his muscled legs and chest. She could have moaned at the sensation but decided to kiss Joseph instead.

She plundered his mouth as he held her close before taking over and commanding the kiss, robbing Sarah of her senses. Her body was on fire with need, her breasts ached, and her core throbbed to a steady rhythm. Everything inside her wanted to mate with Joseph.

His calloused hands only served to heighten her need. Joseph was a man who worked with his hands and trained hard to protect his people. He was an honest man, kind and true, and Sarah wanted him for her own.

"Mate me," Sarah gasped as Joseph used his thumb and index finger to pinch and twist her hard nipples.

"You want to be mine forever?" Joseph asked in a gravelly voice.

"No, I want you to be mine forever," Sarah responded with a growl as her canines extended. "Mine alone."

"Sweetheart, I already am," Joseph said, making her hyena whine with happiness.

Joseph's eyes flashed to amber, his wolf peeking through at her. As every shifter was one with their animal, that animal had to agree with the choice of mate or the shifter would become unbalanced as the two fought for control.

Her hyena was all in, and by the playful growls and protruding fangs, so was Joseph's wolf. Sarah slid her warm, wet body up far enough so that she straddled his hips, allowing his hard cock to press against her sensitive folds.

Joseph skimmed his right palm down the front of Sarah's overheated body until his fingers found that one spot that sent her flying. Fire shot through her veins as her orgasm came from out of nowhere, leaving her panting and moaning her release.

His big hands held Sarah by the waist and lifted her to hover above his cock. "Lead me into you, love, so that we can be mated for all eternity."

That was what Sarah wanted badly, this wonderful man by her side for all time. She reached down and lined up the head of his cock with her core before Joseph slowly lowered her body down, filling her with him.

Sarah felt her body stretch, welcoming her mate inside, feeling every inch of him slide deeper until they were one. The only sound in the steam-filled bathroom was their panting breaths as their gazes locked.

"I love you, Sarah, and swear myself to you in this life and all others," Joseph growled, his canines fully extended, preparing to give her his mating bite.

Sarah ran her tongue over her canines before saying, "I love you, Joseph. We are one in this life and all others."

The moment the words were spoken, the impulse to bite her mate was overpowering, and she yielded to that desire. His sharp teeth pierced her skin moments before Sarah did the same. It felt glorious, like nothing she'd ever imagined or experienced before.

As she drew Joseph's essence into her, and he drew Sarah's into him, their mating bond slammed into place, allowing them to share in each other's pleasure on a whole new level. Their bodies moved as one as each stroke brought her closer to another orgasm. Sarah licked the mating bite closed before Joseph did the same with his. The permanent scar would declare them mated for all to see.

Their kisses became desperate as their bodies wound tighter with every thrust until Sarah's world shattered once again, leaving her screaming her release to the rafters. Soon after, Joseph came with a growl pushing himself deeper inside of her and spreading his seed.

She was well and truly his, and he was hers. That was all that mattered.

Chapter Thirteen

What a difference a day makes.

Sarah felt as if she'd woken in an alternate universe. Shifters she'd never met before were stopping to talk with her and smiling. It was freaking the hell out of her.

"They're just thankful and now realize you are truly one of them," Joseph explained as they continued down the corridor.

"It only took my possible death to make that happen," Sarah half teased. Going from hated to wanted would take some getting used to. After a lifetime of being shunned, this about-face felt jarring.

"Give them time to get to know you for more than saving this facility," Joseph suggested. *"You'll see a change in no time."*

Sarah squeezed his hand in understanding before waving at a small child and his mother across the way. Their smiles were genuine, and Sarah appreciated that.

They'd been called into a meeting with the leaders in the dreaded boardroom. Sarah had hoped to hide out in their apartment for a few days before reappearing, but this meeting had changed those plans. She hoped there wasn't any more bad news the leaders wanted to share with them.

The doors to the boardroom were open when they arrived, so they walked straight in. Both triads, along with Zahra and John, sat waiting for them and ended their conversations when the two of them entered.

"Sarah, Joseph, would you please join us?" Rose asked, indicating the two chairs they'd sat in the first time Sarah had been summoned here.

"Congratulations on your mating," Raz said with a cheer in her tone. "I wish you a long and happy life together."

"It's good to see that you've recovered, Sarah," Axel said with a smile. "We are in your debt for helping to save our new home."

"What you did was amazing," John stated in what sounded like awe.

Sarah knew there had to be more than congratulations involved to have called them here, but she'd wait. "You're welcome." Joseph pulled her chair closer to his own, making her smile.

"We do have a few items that need to be cleared up before we can move forward, as well as news," Mason explained.

John motioned to one of the three Enforcers in the room, and the shifter opened the doors on the far side of the room. Two more Enforcers ushered Rachel and Severn forward, both in chains. Sarah's stomach turned when the venomous woman looked her way.

Joseph gave up on all pretense and lifted Sarah from her chair to put her on his lap. She was thankful for the comfort. Sure, she'd dealt with death when being held prisoner, but the evil radiating from this particular lioness was comparable to any Collector she'd ever met.

"The two of you stand charged with attempted murder and treason," Riker stated as he stood. "What do you have to say for yourselves before we pass judgment?"

Honestly, Sarah was more certain Severn was going to pass out than speak, but Rachel couldn't wait to further endear herself to their leaders.

"You have no right to rule over me," she growled and attempted to lunge onto the table before one of the Enforcers yanked on her chain, pulling her back into position.

Axel leaned back in his chair, steepling his fingers in front of him. "This I have to hear. What makes you believe you are above judgment for your crimes?"

"I'm a lioness. My ancestors ruled over all of you minor shifters for centuries," she announced.

"What history books have you been reading?" Zahra asked, and Sarah wondered as well. She'd never heard of a time where lions ruled anyone.

"I've been taught by the best lion-shifter minds. I've traveled to other prides across the globe, all confirming your history books wrong. My family is powerful, owning half of Los Angeles. We have homes and businesses around the world to watch over our many assets. Lower shifters, like yourselves, don't want the truth to come out that lions are and were always the top species."

Sarah wondered if all lion shifters believed that nonsense and were allowed to have such disrespect for other shifters that they viewed as second rate and beneath them. She'd always thought it was their egos, but to learn they'd been taught this as truth was disturbing.

"You're a sad, misguided lion," Rose said, her compassion for the innocent child Rachel used to be showing for only a moment before she continued. "If I believed there was any way to rehabilitate you, we would have tried, but this ideology goes much deeper than any of us can fix."

The leaders were silent for a moment as they discussed their choices through their private links. Sarah tried to imagine being raised to believe she was better than anyone else. It would be confusing and terrifying when the truth came out that you were no different from anyone.

In retrospect, was Rachel at fault for her beliefs because that was the way she was raised? There was a definite gray area to that argument, but what couldn't be argued was the fact that she'd intended to kill Sarah and endanger every last shifter in the facility. Those were her actions for which she alone was responsible.

When it seemed as though they'd reached a decision and Mason was about to speak, Sarah raised her hand. That was how she'd been taught by her parents to get attention, considering they'd once had a full house of extended family.

Mason looked at her with a smile. "Yes, Sarah. Something you'd like to add?'

Sarah lowered her hand and looked around the room as everyone stared back at her.

"I'd like to suggest a possible punishment." Sarah's voice squeaked, and she tried to clear her throat. *You are strong. You can do this.*

"I know what you want," Rachel sneered. "My head as your trophy, dog."

Raz flicked a finger in Rachel's direction, shutting the disturbing woman's mouth. "We've heard enough out of you."

"Go ahead, sweetheart," Joseph reassured. "Don't ever let someone stop you from speaking your mind, not anymore."

Sarah wanted to hug him but realized the others were waiting for her answer so it would have to wait.

"Rachel is determined to go home to one of her family's houses anyway, so I say we give her what she wants. Send the bird with her."

Raz's green eyes flashed. "I like the way you think."

"Are we all agreed?" Mason asked. At their nods, he continued, "Rachel and Severn, you believe you are capable of surviving on your own, you shall have your chance."

"You have broken our trust and can no longer remain here," Rose growled. "I will teleport the two of you to a house of Rachel's choosing."

"Los Angeles," Severn yelled. "Sand and surf."

Sarah still couldn't believe those two thought they could slip right back into the California way of life. It was no longer the city of angels, and more closely resembled a pit of demons.

"You have been told repeatedly what to expect but choose to ignore our warnings. Once we leave you there, we will not return for you." Rose made the judgment crystal clear.

"Fine, fine. Let's get this over with. I need a drink," Rachel scoffed. "I'll be safer among my kind."

Even now, her belligerence was shocking.

"Very well," Axel said. "Return them to their cells. We will be down to relocate you after our meeting has concluded."

When it looked as if Rachel was going to say something else, Raz silenced her again, for which Sarah was thankful. She would never understand manipulative and evil motivations. All Sarah had ever wanted was to be safe and loved.

"And you are, sweetheart," Joseph whispered into her ear, making chills run down her shoulders and spine.

"Love you too," she replied.

Once Rachel and Severn were taken away, Sarah had no reason to suspect there was more for her to be involved with, so she stood, assuming it was time to leave.

"Sarah, we have something further we'd like to discuss with the two of you," Xander said, causing her to sit back down.

"Is there more news?" Joseph asked.

"Is something wrong?" Sarah naturally went for the worst-case scenario. When was she going to stop that habit?

"Nothing is wrong, but we do have news," Rose said while looking directly at Sarah. "We've received word of an albino hyena being held in a small town in South America close to the Peruvian border with Ecuador."

Sarah couldn't move. She wasn't even sure she was still breathing. Her sister was alive, and they might have found her location.

"We have cougar shifters in the area going in tonight to have a closer look. They're aware of her importance to us and will assist if needed," Mason explained as if the news wasn't shocking and Sarah's world hadn't been turned upside down.

Joseph's arms tightened around her as he took over on her behalf. "How quickly can we move out if it is confirmed she is being held there?"

"Within the hour of confirmation," John answered.

"Do we have the number of enemies on the ground there?" he asked. "What's the make-up? Demons, hunters, and other hyenas?"

"Early reports indicate not as many as we faced at the zoo, but yes, all three were seen on the grounds," Riker answered.

Sarah managed to pull herself together and said, "I want to be there when you go in to rescue her."

Joseph looked at her with concern. "It will be too dangerous for you there. They could try to take you back."

"You don't understand. My sister is powerful, meaning too dangerous for you. With me there, she'll know you're not another group wanting to take control of her power. I'm not sure how they've kept her prisoner this long, but I suspect it has something to do with those collars." It was the only explanation.

"The ones we saw in the meat packing facility?" Xander asked.

"Yes. I wish I'd had a chance to pull one of those apart. They need to be destroyed. The wearer has no free will at all." She knew from personal experience. "That's the only way those evil assholes can control powerful beings."

"Marie had the displeasure of having it used on her before we were able to free her," Zahra said. *"I'd like us to get our hands on one of those to have Sarah and Ben figure it out."*

"Sarah," Raz began. "If your sister is wearing one, do you think you'd be able to disable it if we get you close enough?"

"Wait a minute." Joseph stood with Sarah in his arms. "We were discussing the reasons why she shouldn't be put in danger, and now you want to put her on the front lines."

Sarah could feel his fear and anger with the fact that this was even being considered as she tried to push calm into him.

"Joseph, please sit down," Sarah requested. "It's time for both of us to face a few fears, love."

Her mate didn't look convinced, but he sat back down, which was a start.

"As for your question," she said, "yes, I should be able to revert the collar to its separate base parts if I'm in the same room with it."

"I swear to you, Joseph," Rose said, "we will be by her side the entire time."

"So will I," Joseph growled. The leaders understood the mating bond and didn't take offense to the growl.

"Then that is settled. We will inform the two of you the moment we have word back from the cougar leaders," Mason said.

"Again, Sarah and Joseph, thank you for all you've done for this community, this...." Raz stopped and seemed to be thinking of the right word to use.

"Family," Sarah chose the word that most fit for how she saw things.

"Exactly," Raz agreed. "We are all family."

***

Hours later, Rose followed her mates, Mason and Riker, to the cells. It was sad to hear that these had even needed to be created, but recent events had confirmed their validity.

"Watch your step, love," Riker warned before picking her up. "There's something wet on the floor."

"You're overprotective," she laughed. "I think I can make it through a puddle."

"Yep, I am." Riker chuckled. "As it should be."

Rose simply shook her head. Nothing she said would change her mates' minds about treating her like spun glass, even knowing that she could kick anyone's ass like the goddess she was.

As their triad neared the prisoners, the prisoners stood and approached the bars. "Are you taking me home now? I've waited long enough." The saboteur was eager to leave.

Rose had to check one last time. "Are you sure you know what you're getting yourselves into?"

"Listen, bitch, we had a deal, so don't go reneging on it now," Rachel challenged.

"Well, that certainly makes this decision a lot easier," Rose huffed.

"You are too kind, Matriarch," Rodec, one of the Enforcers, said. "They do not deserve your concern."

Mason wrapped his big arms around her and kissed the side of her head. "My mate is truly kind."

"Can we get this saccharine bullshit over with already?" Rachel complained.

"Everyone join hands," Rose instructed. Neither prisoner was allowed to get near her as her mates stayed by her side. "Rachel, picture the home you wish to be returned to and its location."

The information appeared in her mind, and Rose didn't waste a moment before teleporting them away. Rose, Mason, and Riker, along with Rachel and Severn, arrived at their location, though it didn't quite look the same as in the lioness's memory.

However, off in the distance, the Pacific Ocean was glittering in the sunlight reflecting off the surface. Past the burned-out shells of what Rose assumed to be former mansions and cars were wild animals searching for food and free-roaming horses that looked as if they were once stabled. At least Rachel's house was still standing, even though it had been redecorated in what could be called urban decay chic.

Rose and her mates stepped back, away from what appeared to be a shocked pair of ex-prisoners, and said, "Good luck."

The last thing Rose saw before vanishing was Rachel's mouth opening as if to say something, but alas, it was far too late for more words. When they returned to the compound, the three of them were on the farm level.

"Why are we here instead of our office?" Riker asked as he dug the toe of his boot into the freshly cut grass.

Rose cuddled further into her mates' arms before answering. "Because our guests wouldn't like to live in our office." She pointed into the distance at the three horses racing in the pasture alongside the sheep and cows. "We'll build them a stable, and the children can come for rides."

Mason squeezed her tight. "You can't save them all, mate." Having seen straight through her like he always did. "No matter how hard you try."

"Maybe not, but I could save them at least," Rose said while motioning toward the three new arrivals. "They will be a positive light and bring happiness to others."

"As do you," Riker said.

They watched the horses investigate their new home. The sight gave her renewed hope that their people, having made it through so much in a short amount of time, could come together, no matter what the species, into a cohesive group.

They'd need to be for what lay ahead.

Chapter Fourteen

Joseph couldn't help but smile as he watched Sarah play with Jenny and Matthew while Hope tried to make Gareth go away for what had to be the twentieth time today.

"I don't need you to look out for the children or me. We are fine. The danger is over so you can return to your normal duties." Hope stressed her directive by waving her hands through the air in front of Gareth.

"I have already returned to my position in the machine shop. This is my free time," he replied calmly, never once losing his good-natured grin.

"Why would you spend your free time here?" Hope asked incredulously.

"To assist you as I have given Sarah my word I'd do." Gareth smiled even wider. "We've been over this."

Hope spun around so quickly Joseph was surprised she managed to stay upright, and then she stormed over to Sarah, who smiled at her sweetly from her perch on the purple bear beanbag Marie had brought back for the children. "Tell him he isn't needed here."

"Sorry, he is needed," Sarah replied without elaborating.

"Seriously?" Hope shook her head. "That's your answer?"

"Yep. You can't get mad at me because I'm sweet and kind and saved everybody's butts." Joseph loved seeing her playful side come out.

"Butts." Jenny laughed. "Auntie Sarah said butts."

"That 'saves the day' thing is going to wear out quicker than you think," Hope threatened, but anyone could tell she didn't mean it.

"Are you still happy we met?" Sarah asked.

Hope huffed. "Yeah, but you're pushing it." She then turned back to Gareth. "Fine, if you want to help, grab those bags. You can carry the groceries home." Gareth did as he was asked, and when he returned, he couldn't hide his satisfied smile. "Don't get cocky, I can still send you packing."

Joseph did his best to keep his laughter to a minimum but seeing the big tiger shifter following after Hope was more than he could suppress. As the first chuckle left his mouth, Hope turned.

"Don't think I won't kick your ass, wolf, if I have to," Hope warned.

"So cranky," Joseph said.

"Do you need a nap, Hope?" Jenny asked so innocently that he couldn't hold back his laughter.

Hope threw up her hands and stormed off to the courtyard exit.

"I think I'm wearing her down," Gareth said before racing after her.

Marie came over to join them while Ben continued working on the machine they'd recovered.

"How's he coming along with that?" Sarah asked as she joined them on the patio chairs. The children continued to play with Archie, racing back and forth across the courtyard. Their joyful laughter was floating in the air.

"He's close," Marie explained. "Ben thinks it's only a matter of 'when' not 'if' anymore. Want to tell me why you sent Hope a tiger? Not that I'm complaining, I agree she needs help."

Joseph watched as his mate thought about how much to divulge. "Hope is lonely, and so is Gareth."

"What? With all of us here?" Marie waved her arms around to encompass the restricted section. "She hardly has a minute alone."

"You can be lonely in a crowd of people," Sarah explained. "I know from experience."

"So, you think by throwing them together, they'll heal each other's gaps?" Marie asked incredulously.

"Yep. Even more now that I've seen them together." Sarah laughed. "Hope's got a tiger by the tail, that's for sure." They broke out laughing once again.

"Well, I don't see it, but I trust you know what you're doing, Miss Matchmaker."

"That could be my new profession." Sarah smiled. "There's a lot of single shifters down here. It could be like a service. Shifters come to me searching for that special someone. I can see it now."

"No. No way." Joseph chuckled as he stood and picked his love-obsessed mate up into his arms before heading for their home. "The only romance you need to concentrate on is ours, sweetheart."

Sarah snuggled closer to him and said, "In that case, I'm a specialist."

***

Sarah stood in a room filled with Enforcers and Warriors from the pack and clan. They'd received word that her sister was positively identified in the camp and that the rescue mission was going forward.

Each shifter carried a variety of weapons, from guns and blades to claws and teeth when they shifted. Joseph stood by her side as the leaders addressed the assembled group.

"We will be meeting a team of cougars who will lead us to the compound. When night falls, we'll attack and free as many prisoners as possible. Sarah's sister is our main target, but we'll take as many as we can," Axel explained. "As you know, Sarah's sister is an albino shifter with her own powers. She'll be frightened and possibly combative since she doesn't know who we are. If you do find her first, let us know, and we'll bring Sarah to that location."

"Does anyone have questions?" Mason asked.

At the resounding silence, Sarah's gut clenched. They were going to get her sister back. It had been so long since they'd last seen each other Sarah wondered if her sister had forgotten who Sarah was. She hoped her sister hadn't suffered as Sarah had.

"We'll find her, and bring her here to safety," Joseph said. "After that, we'll work through whatever needs to happen to help your sister heal and adjust."

"How did I ever get so lucky as to find you?" Sarah asked, moving closer to his side.

"I think that I'm the one who should be saying that," he said before pulling her into his arms. "Remember to use your powers if you feel threatened."

That had been a concern of hers. She'd be face-to-face with danger and freeze. They had talked it through, and in the end, she felt more confident in herself once she realized her fear stemmed from having to kill someone. She'd never taken a life and wasn't comfortable with it even after everything she'd been through. However, once Joseph had pointed out areas she could strike that wouldn't be fatal, Sarah was on board. There were others trained to do what was necessary, and she'd leave it to them.

The fact that she was a hyena-shifter adverse to killing only served to make her feel all the weaker.

"It takes much more strength to stay your hand when in battle than to let your blade fly freely," Raz said as she joined them. Considering she was the reincarnated Warrior Goddess Avra, Sarah took her words to heart.

"Are you ready?" Rose asked.

Two of the goddesses would be coming along for this rescue. Zahra would remain here to protect the bunkers while they were gone.

"Yes. This is what I've been hoping for so long," Sarah answered.

"Okay, everyone join together," Raz instructed as she and Rose held out their hands to Sarah. When Joseph wrapped his arms around her, the world turned dark, then moments later they were standing in the Amazon rainforest.

The air was sticky and humid as rain poured down on them. Sarah had never been more thankful for Joseph's combat scenarios, especially right now when it came to choosing appropriate clothing. Her boots sunk into the ground and her rain slicker kept her dry. Their team spread out, and Sarah looked up and noticed hardly any light was making it through the canopy of awe-inspiring trees reaching high into the sky.

Birds called their warnings about the new visitors to their world covered in green. Life flourished around them in all its glory, and Sarah would have found this place joyful if it weren't for the reason they were here.

It was truly amazing to watch the Enforcers and Warriors go off and blend into their surroundings. Others who'd arrived in their shifted forms darted away into the forest. Creatures big and small called this lush place home. Sarah could sense their presence around them.

A soft but intentional snap of a twig alerted them to the arrival of the resident cougar-shifters. Sarah doubted they'd make such a mistake unless intentional.

In contrast, the new arrivals had all shifted into their cats. Some were tawny and other reddish-brown to gray. However, all had a black tip on their tails and bright yellow eyes. A few walked along branches in nearby trees while the rest remained on the ground.

Mason and Axel crossed the distance between them, and as they drew closer, two of the cougars shifted into their human forms, one man and one woman. All four raised their right fists to their hearts as a show of respect to the other leaders.

Joseph tightened his hold around her. "Don't worry, sweetheart. Mason and the cougar alpha are old friends."

Sarah had to admit that did make this entire situation a touch better. With the world in chaos, it wasn't odd for people to turn on one another to survive.

"Sarah, would you please come join us," Mason's voice floated through her mind, making Sarah jump. She wasn't used to being linked to everyone in the community yet, so it surprised her when a random voice spoke up.

Both Goddesses released her hands, and Joseph stepped up to stand beside her. "Okay, sweetheart?"

Sarah took hold of his offered hand and said, "Let's go get my sister."

***

Joseph kept his senses open to any possible threats, but the cougars remained at a respectful distance while the leaders talked. He understood the cougars were taking a risk getting involved, but they too believed shifters needed to band together for the greater good. Until all shifters believed this, chances weren't good that they'd be able to defeat the menace plaguing this world.

Mason went about introducing them when they drew near. "This is Sarah and her mate Joseph. It's her sister whom we've come to free, along with anyone else we might find trapped in there."

"Hello." Sarah's voice was soft but sure. His mate had a backbone of steel that she never seemed to recognize in herself. It didn't matter though. Over time, he would make sure she knew how strong and fearless she truly was.

"Hello, Sarah," the woman said before taking hold of Joseph's mate's offered hand. "My name is Amil, queen of my people, and it's a pleasure to meet you." She then pointed at the man by her side. "This is my mate, Jerrel."

Jerrel took Sarah's hand and said, "Welcome to our part of the rainforest. May I confirm your aura?"

Joseph stepped closer. He wasn't sure what that meant. "What does that involve?" He'd be damned if he'd allow someone to walk around in his mate's mind freely.

Jerrel smiled. "I understand, I wish to protect my mate as well, that is why I ask."

"Is my aura the energy around me?" Sarah asked.

"Yes, young one," Amil answered. "My mate has the ability to confirm your truths and match it with the energy surrounding you. He sometimes sees colors, or lights, and even the odd memory. He will not intentionally access your private memories or thoughts, but they can appear on their own."

"I wish to confirm, in the only conclusive way I know, that you are indeed who you say you are before I risk any more of our people," Jerrel explained, which made sense. They were great leaders protecting their people. If roles were reversed, Joseph would do the same thing.

Sarah squeezed Jerrel's hand and said, "Of course, I would expect nothing less. You must know the truth before we go any further."

Jerrel bowed his head and closed his eyes. Joseph could feel the power transfer, but as long as Sarah wasn't showing any fear or pain, he would remain still. The other cougars watched with piqued interest as if this one moment was the determining factor in their course of action. Which, in essence, it was.

When the cougar leader raised his head to look at Sarah, Joseph could tell the man had seen Sarah's truth.

"Thank you. We will help you in any way possible," Jerrel confirmed. "Your and your sister's powers will be put to good use in battles to come."

"Thank you for helping me get her back," Sarah said. "She is my only blood family member left."

"Bonds between siblings can never be truly broken no matter the distance or time," Amil assured. "You shall see."

With that, more cougars came out of the forest and jumped down from the trees to join them.

Joseph's beautiful and tenderhearted mate was making all this possible.

Chapter Fifteen

As the leaders discussed different points of entry into the compound, the rest waited for night to fall. They'd attack in the cover of darkness so the hunters would have more difficulty seeing them. The hyenas and Collectors would be able to see in the dark, as any shifter could.

Sarah had seen the map of the location, and it reminded her of the zoo. Cages containing shifter prisoners were lined up outside like cargo ready to be shipped. Several of Amil and Jerrel's people were in those cages as well. There were also condors, jaguars, and Andean bears.

There were four buildings in total. One large and set in the back with three smaller ones in the center. From what the cougars could puzzle out, the three grouped buildings were where the guards ate and slept, while the Collectors primarily used the larger one.

Her sister was being held in the larger building. She'd only been seen on a handful of occasions, and each time she'd been forced to wear that damn collar around her neck. Sarah was going to get her hands on one of them before this night was through.

Ben and Marie had come along to help and to test a new device they hoped would disrupt the signal in the death machines if they were being used in this compound. There had been only a few pictures taken to help identify her sister, and those were what Sarah was holding onto now with a death grip.

This had been the first she'd seen of her sister in decades, even if they were only photos. Joseph sat on the trunk of a fallen tree with her perched securely beside him. Sarah was going in as her hyena, which was more agile and considerably faster than her human counterpart. Her first duty was to unlock and open all the cages when they were within range. Then, she'd hunt for her sister.

"I'll be by your side every step of the way, I swear it," Joseph said. "I need you to be prepared in the event your sister doesn't recognize you and that we'll be forced to fight her."

Sarah immediately jumped to the worst-case scenario: they'd kill her sister. But this time she stopped herself and calmly thought about it. No one was here to hurt any of the prisoners. Also, her sister was wearing a collar that altered her free will, which brought up a host of concerns. Though, with all that, Sarah still couldn't bring herself to believe her sister would hurt her.

"I understand your reasoning and concern, and I will keep the possibility in my mind and prepare for it. However, I believe she will not harm me." Sarah had to be honest with her mate; secrets and lies didn't belong in a mating. "I don't know if I'm being hopeful or foolish, but that's how I feel."

Joseph pulled her close and leaned down for a kiss filled with love and passion. When they separated, he said, "Your gentle heart won't allow you to think differently. I hope you're right."

"So do I," she replied.

***

She dug her claws into the fertile soil covered in a blanket of fallen leaves. The deep musty smell of decaying foliage, combined with the rich scent of vibrant blooms, made for a distinct pungent smell. A constant hum from insects, chirping of birds, and other noises she didn't recognize added to the mystery of this magical place.

This was it. Plans were complete, and darkness had fallen. Now they were in position outside the compound, watching the guards as they went about their rounds. All foliage had been stripped bare from the area, and the ground was a mud pit caused by all the individuals walking the area. These creatures had no respect for life, why would they care about nature?

The team could see the usual contingent of human hunters with guns and stalking hyenas making up the group on the exterior. At the same time, any Collectors in residence were holed up inside out of the rain. Being damp hurt the preservation of the demons' host human bodies, so they avoided weather extremes. Water, heat, humidity, cold, the sun, all affected the speed at which the hosts decayed.

That was true until they'd discovered a way of transferring a shifter's life force into themselves. Now, a chosen few remained well preserved at the expense of multiple shifters' lives. The Collectors' intent was clear. They were here to stay, and unless shifters could figure out a way to return them to their side of the veil, the world would be lost.

"The other groups are ready to attack," Axel said through their link. *"Sarah, are we close enough for you to unlock the cages?"*

Sarah sent her power out through the remaining distance until she reached the first cage. *"Yes."*

"Okay, on my order, we charge the compound, and you unlock those cages," Axel confirmed.

"Got it," Sarah was quick to answer.

Joseph, large in his wolf form, moved right up to her side, dwarfing her. *"Have I ever properly thanked you for saving me? For returning my life to me and filling it with love, happiness, and friends?"* Sarah asked.

"You never need to thank me for anything. I love you, Sarah," Joseph said as he rubbed his muzzle against hers.

Everyone went on alert as the countdown began. Sarah couldn't slow her racing heart as the moment came closer. Her sister was within reach.

"Now," Axel yelled.

Sarah sent the command to the cages, and instead of unlocking, they crumbled to pieces until there wasn't a single cage left. She may have used a bit more force than was necessary, but they were free all the same. Teams of shifters poured into the compound as gunfire broke out, but Sarah and Joseph stayed the course, heading directly for the largest building.

Rose and Raz followed them up to the front doors, where demons were waiting for them. In a display of raw power, Raz sent a bolt of lightning through the first few hosts, and Rose's wolf grew to ten times her average size.

"We'll take care of them. You go look for your sister," Raz ordered as her lightning cleared a path into the building.

Sarah didn't even break stride beside Joseph as they burst through and into a warehouse-type facility. Metal walls and rafters were all that was visible from their location. Hallways snaked out in three different directions as Joseph looked to her for a decision.

She centered herself, trying to sense her sister, blood calling to blood. All at once, the location screamed at her, and she took off down the far left hallway. Her sister was down this way somewhere.

***

Joseph lunged at the hyena who was charging toward Sarah, and raked his claws across its throat, taking it down. The farther they got into the building, the more resistance they were encountering. Behind them, the rest of their team had already taken control of the exterior and were rushing into the building as well. Joseph could hear the constant flow of information being shared through their link.

He spied a hunter perched in a stairwell with his gun aimed, but before he could knock Sarah out of the way, the metal staircase fell to pieces, sending the hunter and his rifle down two stories.

"Nice catch, sweetheart." Joseph cheered Sarah's quick response. He wanted his mate to use everything at her disposal if necessary.

As they passed what looked to be a laboratory with cages and staff, Sarah dismantled the entire room, freeing the shifters so they could fight back on equal footing—all without slowing her trek to her sister.

Another hyena appeared, but instead of fighting them, it ran in the other direction, somehow knowing the battle was already lost and searching for a way to escape. At the end of the hallway stood a room with closed double doors, and seconds before Sarah could go charging in, Joseph stopped her.

"What are you doing? My sister is in there. I can feel her."

"Sarah, this door is unguarded for a reason. They want us to go in there." They'd fought every step of the way, and to now be faced with no resistance screamed trap.

She stopped for a moment before saying, *"We need to find another way."*

"Exactly." Joseph charged off down an adjacent hallway while informing the others to be cautious of what they suspected waited for them behind that door.

When they reached the far end of the secondary hallway, Joseph stopped and examined a metal seam. *"Sarah, can you silently move the metal off to the side about an inch so that we can look inside?"*

"Yes," she said, and moments later, the thin piece of metal moved aside.

Joseph scanned the interior, finding a single Collector demon standing in the center of a room that was covered in metal pieces with a small white hyena chained to the floor by shackles. The collar was still around her neck as she stared listlessly at the doorway they would have gone through. Who knows what that demon had prepared for them when they entered?

Plans were being made on the fly. Leaders were taking up a position on the far exterior side of the room, away from the front doors, getting ready to storm it.

That was when the building began moving.

***

Sarah watched as metal walls pulled away like giant arms opening wide to reveal the entire team to the Collector and her sister.

The Goddesses held a shield around the shifters on their side of the room as pieces of wood, metal, and concrete rained down upon them. Sarah and Joseph remained unnoticed as they hid themselves behind what was left of a knee wall in what looked to be an office.

"I told you my sister was powerful," Sarah said. *"We have to get that collar off her neck. She has no free will."*

The ground trembled as metal, furniture, containers, and more joined together into giant creatures looming on either side of their remaining team members.

"Inanimate objects to life. Got it," Joseph ground out while placing her farther underneath him for protection. *"We need a distraction so that you can remove her collar."*

"Welcome to my facility," the Collector said as if he were lord of the manor and wasn't surrounded. "We weren't prepared for visitors, but nonetheless there are enough cages for you all."

"Insane or stupid?" Joseph asked.

"Guys, Rose is trying to pull the demon from the host, but she can't get a read on him with our shields in place," Raz said. *"And I can't release the shield while these beasts are hovering over us."*

"I'll cause a distraction," Joseph said. *"Then you can lower the shields while Sarah tries to reach her sister."*

"Understood," the leaders agreed.

"But you'll be in danger. My sister won't be able to stop from doing as the demon requests." Sarah couldn't send him out there to be a target. *"You can't go."*

"It's the only chance we have. With the shields up, Raz and Rose can't even teleport the group to safety. I have to. It's what I've been trained to do."

"Please be safe," Sarah could feel tears gathering in the corners of her eyes. *"I don't want to go on without you."*

"You won't have to," Joseph said as he moved into position. *"See you soon, sweetheart."*

Joseph's wolf took off along the edge of the room, capturing everyone's attention. Steel spikes formed out of scrap metal on the floor, ensuring Joseph wouldn't make it far. Sarah shifted to human, rose from her hiding spot, and screamed, "Stop, sister."

Not only did her sister stop, but everything around them did as well. The spikes remained floating in the air but no longer progressing forward, so that was something. The beasts froze in their positions as the Collector demon's mouth opened in shock.

Sarah tried to dismantle the collar around her sister's neck, but it wouldn't budge; she needed to move closer. With her hands out to her sides, showing that she wasn't a threat, Sarah stepped forward and into the room.

She glanced over at her mate, who was now surrounded by spikes. The rest of her friends remained sheltering under Raz's shield. This wasn't good.

"Who the hell are you?" the demon asked once he managed to speak.

"I'm her sister, and I'm here to take her back." Sarah spoke calmly, never taking her eyes off the hyena so similar to her own.

The demon laughed. Macabre to watch considering the host's lips didn't move. Sarah ignored him and spoke directly to her sister.

"It's me, your sister. I've come to take you to safety." Sarah raised her right hand and held it out to her.

"Destroy them all, I command you," the demon yelled at the snow-white hyena staring back at Sarah.

"I've missed you so much. Please come back with me." Sarah couldn't stop the tears from falling. She didn't care if it made her seem weak. "That's my mate, Joseph. Could you please remove the spikes around him?"

The spikes trembled before falling to the ground.

"Thank you, sister. Joseph gave me my name. It's Sarah. I would love for us to have our naming celebration together. You can choose your name."

"It'll happen," Joseph said, and Sarah turned around to see he'd shifted as well. "You tell us what to do, and it will be done."

"Well, isn't this fucking sweet, a family reunion, complete with Goddesses and the riffraff," the Collector demon growled while waving his arm in the direction of the group of shifters from their team. "Do as I have ordered and destroy them all, including your sister."

Sarah could see lights flickering along the collar's edge, no doubt exerting pressure on her sister to obey.

"I love you, sis," Sarah said. "We promised never to forget each other."

Unfortunately, the Collector ran out of patience, pulled a gun from under his coat, and fired it at Sarah. Time slowed as Joseph shifted to race to her before the bullet did, but he'd never make it. She tried to exert control over the projectile, but it was moving too fast for her.

Sarah closed her eyes and waited for the impact, but it never came. She opened her eyes as Joseph took her into his arms. When she looked back at her sister and the Collector, the demon lay motionless on the ground with a hole in his chest and spikes peppering its human host body.

"Did you do that?" Joseph asked without releasing his hold on her.

"No." Sarah hadn't thought of the spikes lying on the ground.

A black mist rose from the host body. The demon was desperate to escape, but Rose was waiting for him. The second he was free, the Goddesses pulled him inside a floating cube of light before it vanished, never to be seen again.

Sarah ran to her sister's side, reached for the collar, and transformed it back into its original separate parts, freeing her. Burn marks peppered the skin around the small hyena's neck, proof of the pressure the collar was exerting on her. Sarah couldn't help but wrap her arms around her sister and cry. Sarah had her sister in her arms again.

Though Sarah still couldn't reach her through using their sister bond, it didn't matter. It would all come back in time.

When she didn't shift, Sarah understood why. Her sister was confused and frightened, both emotions familiar to Sarah as well. "It'll be okay now. You're safe. I promise."

Joseph stood guard over them as her sister rested her hyena's head on Sarah's lap and whined, breaking Sarah's heart. This was how she had begun her journey with Joseph. Sarah would do the same thing Joseph had done for her, show her sister the love she'd been missing and all the support she needed.

Sarah had been lucky to have her mate by her side through it all, and she would never forget that. She had her mate, and now her sister.

Sometimes, prayers got answered.

Chapter Sixteen

Joseph sat in the courtyard watching as Archie, the golden retriever, chased after a pillow puppy. Yes, a puppy made out of throw pillows was running back and forth as fast as the real thing. The children thought it was terrific having two dogs, and Hope was happy only to have to clean up after one.

Sarah's sister sat in the bay window of their apartment much the same as Sarah had done. Other than animating toys for the children, she hadn't felt comfortable enough to come out or shift yet. They'd connected the apartment next to theirs so that the new arrival had her own space while being close to Sarah.

Everyone in the area made a point of waving and speaking to her on their way by so that she'd feel like part of the group.

Ben and Sarah were working on the collar they'd brought back, but there hadn't been one of those machines of death on the property when they'd searched. Ben hadn't been able to test out his theory on one of the active devices, but knew many more opportunities would come, unfortunately.

Joseph's mate stood from the table and smiled at him as she came closer. His heart always skipped a beat when Sarah smiled or did anything, really. He never realized how much he could love one person until he'd met his mate.

"Want some company?" Sarah asked as she approached his side.

"Always, as long as it's you," Joseph replied as he moved over on his lounger, making room for her to join him. Once Sarah was settled, he pulled her close and began running his fingers through her soft white hair. "How goes the work on the collar?"

"Better than I'd hoped," she said with a great deal of excitement. "Now that we have one to examine, Ben believes he has an idea on how we could turn them off remotely."

"That's great news," Joseph said. "When do you guys start trials?"

"Once we find someone willing to put it on," Sarah said while batting her long pale eyelashes at him.

"Oh no. Not a chance that thing's going around my neck. What about Gareth?" Yeah, Joseph was all for helping, but that was one step too far for him.

"Not a chance, Hope is liable to tell Gareth to jump off something."

"What about Ben?"

"He's the one doing the testing."

"Wait, I'll contact Solomon. He owes us."

"You're willing to sacrifice your younger brother?" Sarah asked while trying not to laugh.

"Hell yeah."

Sarah's laughter was a balm to his soul. Her joy was infectious and changed his entire perspective on everything.

Truth be told, Sarah had saved him, more than Joseph had saved her. One day he hoped they'd have their own children when the world was at peace again.

He'd hold that dream close and accept nothing less.

This war was far from over.

ABOUT THE AUTHOR

Lilli Carlisle lives in the country near Toronto, Canada. She is the mother of two wonderful girls, wife to an amazing man, and servant to the pets in her life, and she's a member of Toronto Romance Writers. Lilli writes paranormal romance, and believes love should be celebrated and shared. After all, everybody needs a little romance, excitement, intrigue, and passion in their lives.

Connect with Lilli:

Instagram:/lillicarlisle

facebook.com/lillicarlisleauthor

twitter.com/LilliCarlisle

www.BOROUGHSPUBLISHINGGROUP.com

If you enjoyed this book, please write a review. Our authors appreciate the feedback, and it helps future readers find books they love. We welcome your comments and invite you to send them to info@boroughspublishinggroup.com. Follow us on Facebook, Twitter and Instagram, and be sure to sign up for our newsletter for surprises and new releases from your favorite authors.

Are you an aspiring writer? Check out www.boroughspublishinggroup.com/submit and see if we can help you make your dreams come true.

www.ingramcontent.com/pod-product-compliance
Lightning Source LLC
Chambersburg PA
CBHW071316130626
46556CB00004B/1631